By: Jordan Marie

Formatting Services: Paul Salvette & BB eBooks

Cover:
Designer: Margreet Asselbergs – Rebel Edit Designs
Model: Antonio Clyburn
Photographer: Shauna Kruse of Kruse Images & Photography Models & Boudoir
Picture of Woman: Shutterstock
(Stock Photo used on the back of paperback only)

Trademarks:

The Content in this book is intended for mature audiences only. 18+ and above.

Contains violence, sexual situations, excessive profanity, and death. Reader should please read with that knowledge. Please do not read if any of the above offends you.

Previous Titles in the Series

Skye

The minute I saw him, I knew I was in trouble. *Bull.*

What kind of man flirts with the doctor who lectures him on STD's?

And why am I attracted to a man like that?

He wasn't what I wanted, but he could be exactly what I need.

Slowly I'm learning to trust him.

It's perfect, except for one small thing....

Someone wants me dead.

Bull

To say I lost my way is an understatement.

Then I meet her. *Skye.*

She's smart, beautiful and way beyond my reach.

It doesn't matter, I'm keeping her.

I know what I want and I go after it.

Now someone is trying to take her away from me.

I won't let that happen.

She's mine and I'm not giving her up.

TABLE OF CONTENTS

Dedication

To Bo. My best friend, my heart, my companion. I miss you more every minute that goes by. You were my best friend. The ten years with you went too quickly. Rest easy my friend. Until we meet again…

Note From the Author

Dear Readers,

I hope you enjoy Trusting Bull. I was supposed to get Captured out in December, but Bull wouldn't quit talking. This story is different than the other Savage Brothers' stories, but hopefully you give Bull & Skye a try.

I feel out of touch with some of my readers because life has been so hectic. I wanted to take this opportunity to tell you that you helped make this year one of the best I've ever had in my life.

You have my thanks and my love, for taking a chance on me. I hope you stick around to see what's coming up in 2016. I'm excited to share not one but two new series with you.

Happy Reading & Merry Christmas
Jordan

Prologue

SKYE

I LOOK AT the man on my exam table. I shouldn't be attracted to him. I mean he's good looking, so he would catch any woman's eye. He's tall and has arm porn that would make any woman weak in the knees. He's got an aura of danger about him and a bad boy vibe that goes on for miles. That's not why I shouldn't be interested in him though. No, that reason is pretty much summed up in one sentence.

"You have gonorrhea, Mr. Kane."

"That's not fucking possible."

"I'm afraid it is, the good news, is that despite your lapse in judgment, it is curable. However, I would suggest we test you for other sexually transmitted diseases including HIV."

"I don't fucking have AIDS lady."

I frown at his reply. It's not the first time I've dealt with a belligerent patient, but after working for thirty-six hours straight, I'm just not in the mood.

"Mr. Kane, have you or have you not been having sex?"

"Yes *doctor*, but I always wrap my shit up. So I'm telling you, your goddamn diagnosis is wrong. Now how about you get your ass out there and find me someone who knows what the fuck they are doing around here."

I hold my head down and let out a big breath. I rub the

tension headache starting at my temple. I really should have tried to do my residency in New York. I stupidly thought the small town atmosphere of London, Kentucky was what I wanted.

I'd like to say my next actions are because I am tired, or the fact that I'm on my period. I'd also like to think it is because of this patient's crappy attitude. Still, I know the truth. The truth is Mr. Kane hit a sore spot. I'm vain enough to admit it. His words are startling similar relate to the chewing out the chief resident gave me this morning. The reason I was hauled onto the carpet wasn't my fault, but a mistake made by a nurse. Yet, since the resident in question is busy banging said nurse, I took the hit. So, with Mr. Kane's words, I can't hold back. I don't even try. *I snap.*

"I do know what I'm doing. I absolutely know, Mr. Kane. The fact that you've had sex with someone who has gonorrhea, upped your chances of getting the disease. Now if you did in fact *wrap it up,* then possibly you didn't when you gave or received oral sex. Perhaps you had one night of drunken sex and forgot to *wrap your shit up,* as you so colorfully stated. I do not know how or with whom you transmitted the disease. What I do know is that you have, in fact, contracted gonorrhea, or more commonly referred to as the clap, if that helps. So what's going to happen, Mr. Kane, is simple. You can keep a civil tongue in that pretty boy head of yours when speaking to me and be thankful that you do just have gonorrhea, or you can leave. Now, I will warn you, should you choose to leave, that foul discharge that you've kept hidden that keeps leaking out of your penis, will only get worse. That burning sensation you have when you urinate, will only increase. Those swollen glands along your neck, will only get worse. What I suggest you do instead, Mr. Kane, is man up."

He looks at me strangely. I can't say as I blame him. In fact, had my chief resident walked in during my speech, I would be in major hot water. However, he didn't and I'm tired, plus Mr. Kane is the last patient that stands before me and a much needed three days off. So instead of practicing caution, I forge ahead.

"Pretty boy?" He asks. "Did you just call me a pretty boy?"

"I told you to step up. Take your medicine like a grown man, without belittling those of us who are trying to ensure that you receive quality medical care. Take tests to confirm you don't have something worse and, finally, make a list of your sexual partners to determine where you contracted the disease and make sure they get treated so that the cycle ends."

"You just called me pretty boy," he repeats and I try not to blush.

That was probably going a step too far. Well, in actuality, the entire speech was going too far. If he files a complaint, I am most likely through here. I'm not sure I care at this point.

"Mr. Kane, honestly, it's late. I'll have the nurse come in to give you a shot, and I'll need you to follow up with your family physician…"

"Your eyes sparkle, when you're mad."

"I really…what did you say?"

"I said, your eyes sparkle, when you're mad," he repeats.

"Are you seriously…you're *hitting* on me?"

"Is that so hard to believe?" He asks as he leans back in the chair and I think that perhaps I've lost it. It's definitely past time for me to go home.

"Considering I just told you that you have a venereal disease and the fact that I am your doctor, oddly enough, Mr. Kane, I do find it hard to believe."

"I don't happen to believe you, but even if what you say is

true, I take the meds you give then I'm good right?"

I'm at a loss. I choose to ignore the part about him hitting on me. Hopefully after tonight, I won't see him again. So, I concentrate instead on the only thing that matters.

"Providing you make sure the woman or women you have been having sexual relations with are treated, then yes."

"Sexual relations? C'mon Doc, let's call what it is. Fucking."

At his explicit words, I feel heat creep into my face and it annoys me. I'm not a prude for God's sake, it's just this is not the type of conversation I would choose to have with a patient.

"Regardless of what you call it, you need to contact them and find the source."

"You're telling me to get a list of names of everywhere I've stuck my dick? Hell, I can't remember that, Doc. It's impossible."

"The symptoms have a limited gestation period, so really the last three weeks to be..."

"That's impossible," he says again interrupting me and I'm taken back. *Seriously?*

"You can't remember who you've had sex with in the last *three* weeks?"

He shrugs, "Not really, no."

"Of course you can't," I mumble, without meaning to. What were my original thoughts of this man? Yeah, scratch that, I'm definitely *not* attracted now. "Regardless Mr. Kane, that is for you and your doctor to discuss. I will of course give you a shot of antibiotics tonight. Your primary care physician can further treat you when you follow up."

"Excuse me, Dr. Walker, I heard my boyfriend was here. Oh, Bull baby, are you okay? I told you, you should see a doctor about that cold. How about I take you to my place and make you some soup and…"

I'm frozen as the whore of St. Lutheran's Hospital walks through the door—otherwise known as Nurse Melissa Allen. The very nurse who was responsible for my ass chewing earlier tonight. Of course she's this guy's girlfriend. *Of course.* The only bright spot I can find in this scenario is that perhaps Melissa has also passed along the gift of love to Dr. Eldrdige. It really couldn't happen to a nicer guy.

"I take it you two know each other?" I sarcastically add since she's about to smother him in her breasts. To his credit, Mr. Kane pulls away from her and looks more annoyed than anything.

"We've been dating for the last three months," Melissa pipes up proudly.

"Odd, I thought you were dating Dr. Eldridge," I say, marking the medication orders down in the chart, ready to get out of there.

"We're not exclusive," Nurse Allen says.

"We're not dating, we're just fucking," Mr. Kane says, almost at the same exact time.

"I see. Well then, I'm sorry Nurse Allen but you probably should be tested for gonorrhea and, in fact, you should ask Dr. Eldridge also."

She gasps and steps back like I slapped her. *Oh if only I could.*

"What did you say?"

"It would appear your boyfriend…"

"We're not dating. We're just fucking," Mr. Kane interjects again, and I want to laugh when Melissa shoots him a dirty look.

"It would appear Mr. Kane has contracted the STD. For the sake of your health, you should also be tested. I can order it done now if you'd like?" I say and I try to keep the glee out of my voice. I would *love* to ask the hospital tech to run the tests. It would be so much fun to watch it filter through the hospital grapevine.

"That's not necessary, there's no way that I have the clap! And if you mention this to anyone, I will make sure that your supervisor…"

"Shut it, Melissa. I think I want you tested," Mr. Kane interjects.

"I will not," she counters.

"You will if you want to step foot back in the club."

Really this could almost be fascinating if I had any sleep. I haven't, and I desperately hate being anywhere near Nurse Allen. So I decide to extricate myself from the situation.

"Well, you two can discuss this later. I'll have one of the nurses come in to give you your shot, Mr. Kane, and to discharge you. Please make sure you follow up with your doctor."

"Oh I will. Don't you worry about that," he says and he seems to be smiling a lot for a man who has just been diagnosed with an STD.

I close the door and take a deep breath. Dr. Torres is already being handed charts. I'm officially off duty. *Hallelujah!*

Chapter 1

SKYE

One Week Later

"YOU'RE LOOKING GOOD tonight, Doc."

His voice stops me. I hold my head down and breathe out the moment of fear he caused in me. Then I pinch the bridge of my nose, between my eyes and think again for the hundredth time... *Why me?*

"Mr. Kane, this is getting to be a habit," I tell him as I turn and lean on my car. He walks closer and doesn't stop until he's right in front of me. One of his hands rests on my car door, effectively boxing me in as leans down and gives me a smile.

It should be illegal for a man to look this good. Dark mocha skin reminds me of another weakness I have: hot chocolate. So sinfully enticing that I want to lick every inch of him to see if he's just as sweet. His dark eyes always seem to glow and tonight competes with the diamond stud he's wearing in his right ear. His body is chiseled to perfection and he's a walking billboard-ad for Wrangler jeans. His head is shaved completely bald. I've shamefully imagined holding it while he works between my legs. He's wearing a white t-shirt under his leather cut that proclaims him part of the Savage Brothers' Motorcycle Club. There's a patch under his nickname that says Enforcer and that should just be reason number nine hundred and ninety-nine why I should get in my car and run. Not have fantasies about him, like I have from day one. What kind of woman, let alone a professional woman—a doctor completing her residency—already with too much on her plate, daydreams and fantasizes about a man she diagnosed with the clap? *A woman who needs therapy, sex, or possibly both.* I should be searching for therapists and accepting Dr. Reynolds' invites out to dinner.

Unfortunately, I'm not that smart. I haven't been since I met him in the emergency room. Because here I am, one week after diagnosing him with the clap, standing in a parking garage at the butt-crack of dawn, engaging in a conversation with my own personal stalker. Again. This is becoming a regular thing… every other day, just like clockwork, he's here waiting for me, boxing me in against my car, talking to me. Flirting, invading my space, making me feel alive, making me get a little more addicted to his smile, his humor and to his pres-ence…that's what he's doing. I should run screaming, but instead I find myself flirting back. Like I said, *I'm not that smart.*

"I told you to call me Bull," he reminds me, letting a finger from his free hand twirl in one of the loose tendrils of my hair.

Once again, I shore up my defenses, which admittedly, are weak around him.

"I remember," I tell him, turning away and tucking under his arm so I can open the driver's side door of my car.

He takes the door out of my hand and holds it. I look over my shoulder at him, already knowing I wouldn't make my escape that easily.

"Then why do you keep calling me Mr. Kane?" he asks. In our previous meetings he just says hi, tells me I'm pretty, flirts, and lets me go. Leaving me just thinking about him and fantasizing—like an idiot. Apparently tonight, it's not going to be that easy. *This could be bad.*

"Because we're not friends. I'm the doctor who gave you bad news, and you're the man crazy enough to date a nurse I work with. A nurse I'm not real fond of and, therefore, I don't think I should be calling her boyfriend by his first name. Or, you know, even talking to her boyfriend. So, if you'll excuse me...."

"Sweetheart I don't think I've ever been anyone's *boyfriend* and I sure as hell ain't going to start in my thirties. I'm a man." He says that like I have any doubt.

"Fine, dating. Whatever."

"I told you I wasn't dating Melissa. We were just fucking."

"Yes well, that's just reason number one thousand."

"One thousand?" he asks, and I curse my big mouth for the slip. I'm too tired to be talking to this man.

"One of a thousand reasons I should call hospital security instead of humoring you. If you don't mind Mr. Kane, I'm exhausted. I'm going to go home, kiss Matty and sleep," I tell him, sliding behind the wheel of my car. I can't close the door though, because the damn man won't let go of it. I wonder if I started beating my head on the steering wheel would he feel sorry for me and let me go home?

"Is Matty your old man?" he asks.

"If I say yes, will you leave me alone?"

"Depends on if you're telling the truth," he answers, watching me.

"He's my son," I sigh out my answer. "My very young son, who hasn't seen his mom in over twenty-four hours now. It'd be great if you would move so I could close my door and go home. That'd be really good."

"You got a kid?"

Why didn't I think of this sooner? All men run when they

find out you have a readymade family. Apparently even man-whore semi-stalkers.

"Yes. So you can see, you're wasting your time with me."

"I don't think so. I like that you have a kid. In fact, Doc, I'm liking everything I learn about you."

With that I do bang my head against the steering wheel. Just once, *but still…*

"Did you learn the part where I don't date men who would have anything to do with people like Nurse Allen? Or, who are so careless with their health that they get a venereal disease and then can't remember the names of the mountains of women with whom they've had sex with in a *very short,* three-week period?"

"Cute, Doc. But I didn't ask you out on a date. I'm not really the dating type."

"Oh yes, I forgot. You skip that part and go straight into sleeping with a woman."

"Fucking. There was never any sleeping going on. Women get all weird you start letting them stay in your bed."

"Unbelievable," I mutter and start my car up. I'll just drive off and drag him until he lets go of the door if I have to.

"You know what you should be asking, Doc?"

"I'm afraid to ask."

"Ask me how many women I've fucked since I met you."

"Mr. Kane…"

"Not a damn one," he says, interrupting me. "My dick wants you. And you, Doc? I think you'd be different. You I'd like to date. I think I'd even like sleeping with you."

"That's not going to happen," I tell him ignoring the small thrill that runs through me. I really need to start therapy soon. I have to be close to breaking with reality. That can be the only explanation for this madness.

"Why? You can deny it all you want, Doc, but you're attracted to me. Your nipples are so hard right now, they're about to burst through your shirt."

"That's because it's cold out here, and you're not letting me close my dang car door!" I'm only partially lying, but he doesn't need to know that.

"Whatever you say, Doc."

"Mr. Kane…"

"Tell me why you won't go out with me and I'll let you go."

"I think I've already made that clear, but since those other one thousand reasons haven't penetrated, how about the fact that I got your toxicology reports back, and I know about the drugs that you have in your system? Or how about the fact that your eyes are dilated right now? So, even if I am…*were* attracted to you, you would never be someone I would date. I have my health, my career and my son to think about. I can't afford to make bad decisions, like dating someone who could potentially put my health, career or child in jeopardy. *You*, Mr. Kane, are a walking poster boy for bad dating decisions. Now, if you'll excuse me, I'm going home to my son."

He stands away from the door and a look moves over his face that I can't quite figure out. I want to take my tirade back because I think it hurt him. I won't do that, however, and it doesn't change the truth in what I said anyway. I take off, leaving Mr. Kane in my rearview mirror—exactly where he belongs.

Chapter 2

BULL

I STAND AND watch until her taillights blend into the early morning fog. It shouldn't surprise me the doctor knows I've been popping pills. *It does.* I thought about trying to defend myself, but there really isn't a defense to give. This is the part where I should turn away and not think about Dr. Skye Walker again. But, I find that I can't do that.

Something about this woman makes me feel alive in ways I've never experienced before, even when I thought I was falling for Carrie. Carrie had more to do with wanting to protect and care for her. Skye challenges me. The problem is, I've dug myself into such a large hole that I'll never be able to crawl out of it to even see what this woman could possibly be to me. An overwhelming feeling hits me square in the stomach, like a punch, and I know exactly what it is—*regret.* This woman could have been my future and I've ruined it.

I need to make some big changes if I want to try and pursue something with her—or even just try to get her to talk to me. I rub the back of my neck hard. It's another of those fucking headaches coming on. I feel it starting and just like always I'm helpless to stop it. Here's where I'd take a pill to dull it. Here's where I'd go lose myself in the pills, booze and maybe a woman, before trying to sleep it off. I reach in the pocket of my jeans and take out the small brown bottle. The medicine inside rattles and the sound is a siren's call, beckoning me to take just one more taste.

I start to do that very thing until I remember the look of disgust on Skye's face as she called me on it. She's a good woman—a strong woman. She's the type of woman a man could hold on to and never worry about what the future holds. *She's a woman worth trying for.*

That's the thing right there. I haven't felt like getting out of bed in so fucking long, let alone trying. Skye changes that. I palm the bottle in my hand and tighten it up. I can feel the plastic bending under the weight of my grip. I sit down on the concrete ledge that separates section A from this one. I put the pills beside me and stare at them while I dial my phone.

It takes three rings before the sleepy sounding voice answers, "Hello?" she asks, sounding confused.

"I need a favor," I tell her straight out, not beating around the bush.

"Who is it?" I hear Crush in the background saying. "It's just Nic, go back to sleep Cowboy," she says before her voice comes back to the receiver. Her voice is stronger now, clear and definitely wide-awake. "Let me go into the bathroom. I don't want to disturb, Zander."

I keep staring at the pills, alternating between being afraid of what I'm about to do and afraid of *not* doing it. I place my free hand on my leg and watch as it shakes. I don't think it has anything to do with the occasional tremors I have. I hear a door close through the phone and then Dani's voice comes back to me.

"What do you need, Bull?" she asks, her voice laced with concern. Dani has gone through a lot of changes since she and Crush worked shit out. I hated her once. Part of me still might.

But she was the only one who saw me sinking. She was the only one who reached out a hand. I still remember the last time I saw her before she and Crush left to join Diesel's crew in Tennessee. She hugged me, which frankly scared the hell out of me. Dani and I didn't have that kind of relationship. I never wanted one with her. I blamed her for all kinds of shit, even if most of it wasn't her fault. She made mistakes that hurt people I loved and, therefore, that made her someone not worth my time. Saying that now makes me an asshole, because the mistakes I made aren't exactly minor and I don't have the reasons behind them like Dani did.

"You didn't have to lie to him," I tell her, stalling. My voice is gruff, and I can almost taste my own fear. Hell, Skye was right to look at me with disgust.

"Did you want me to tell him the truth?" she asks, because she knows why I'm calling. She knows because on that last day when she hugged me she pressed a note in the palm of my hand. I waited until I was alone to read it, and I was glad I did.

I know what you do when you think no one sees. I see the emptiness in you because I've lived it. If you ever need a friend, I'm here. Call me.

I destroyed the note, but I stored the number she scribbled at the bottom into my phone. I've never used it, never even thought about it, until Skye threw my drug test results in my face. Now I sit here facing the fact that I've lost a shot at a good woman because of what I've become.

Realistically I knew it would be hard to get close to Skye with the damned way we met the first time between us. I always suit up. *Always.* Except for that one night when I was higher than a kite and feeling no pain. Melissa went down on me and a condom on my cock was the last thing I thought about when she took me into that wet mouth of hers and sucked me like a damn vacuum cleaner.

I rake my hand over the back of my neck and hold it there. Hoping the warmth staves off some of the pain.

"Bull?" Dani questions again and, shit, I wonder how long I've had her on the phone, not talking.

"Not really, I guess," I answer clearing my throat. "I...fuck I don't know why I'm calling."

"Yeah you do."

"Yeah, I guess I do," I tell her hating the defeat in my voice.

"It's good you called, Bull."

"You think?" I joke, thinking it's anything but good.

"Yeah, it means you're tired of falling."

Falling. Yeah that's a good term for it.

"So what now?" I ask her because I don't know what I thought she could do from another state away, but I just know I don't have the first clue of what to do on my own.

"We find you help."

"I thought that's what you were supposed to be? My help, I mean."

"You need meetings, Bull. You need sobriety. I'm an ear and someone who's been where you're at right now. I'm a sounding board that's not here to judge. I'd like to say friend, but I don't have to be. I can be your sponsor if you'd rather."

"Sponsor?"

"Yeah, I have one. Though honestly, Zander is my rock these days. Still, there are times when I need to reach out to Leslie."

I take a deep breath. "So, sponsor, where do we go from here?"

Her voice comes back to me and it's one word, but I hear

her happiness in it and I hold onto it. She's a woman who lived without happiness for so long. She had every reason to give up. If she can find it, maybe I can, too.

"Up," she says. "We go up, Bull."

I take a breath. Then another. I stand up, grab the bottle and walk to the large trashcan in front of the elevators.

"I want to try," I tell her and throw the pills in the garbage.

"That's the hardest step to take, Bull."

She's not lying. It does feel that way. I hope this doesn't end up being another thing I fail at.

Chapter 3

SKYE

Three Months Later

I LOVE THE mountains in Kentucky. I love everything about them. From their large rolling views to the way they make you feel sheltered and protected—almost as if you were in God's arms. They grabbed my attention years ago and never let go. It's the main reason I decided to settle here with Matty. They're gorgeous any time of the year—from Spring, when new growth takes place and different hues of green call to you, to Autumn, when trees set off a display of colors that no firework show could match. They hold so much beauty it takes my breath away. They all pale in comparison to what I'm looking at now, however. It's a beautiful day, and I decided to have lunch on the cement picnic tables out from the courtyard of the hospital. It's relatively empty, because most of the hospital staff likes to congregate in the food court area. I hate crowds, so this suits me better. The fact that Mr. Kane is staring down at me right now leaves me torn between wondering if I shouldn't run back towards to the food court or ask him to sit down. I haven't seen him in three months. I thought our last encounter had chased him off, and it was for the best. I shouldn't have missed him—*but I did*, and not seeing him made me sad.

"Mr. Kane."

"Hey Doc, did you miss me?" he asks, and he's smiling and clearly joking but something about him is different.

"Was I supposed to?"

"Ouch, Doc, that hurts," he says sitting down.

"Have a seat," I tell him, sarcastically.

"What is that you're eating?" he says, curling up his nose.

I can't say as I blame him. I look down at my sad chicken wrap and drop it back onto the plate.

"I think it's a new concoction the hospital cafeteria is working on in case of a zombie apocalypse."

"Zombie apocalypse?"

"Yeah something they freeze dried for a year, and it was supposed to keep. Only I don't think it did. Oh well, I wasn't real hungry."

"Now that's a shame, Doc because I come bearing gifts," he says and it's then that I notice he's holding a paper bag and a drink carrier. I missed it before because the man is so fine, I find myself glued to his beautiful eyes and then the way his t-shirt likes to cling to that stomach. It's no wonder I fantasize about him. *I'm only human after all.*

He puts his items on the table and reaches in and brings out two wrapped sandwiches and hands me one along with a large coffee.

"What are you doing?"

"Having lunch with you? I didn't know how you liked your coffee so I got it black, but there's some creamer and shit in the bag if you want it."

I look at him like he's grown two heads. I haven't seen or heard from him since our last run in, and I'm not sure what I thought would happen if I saw him again. *Fantasies don't count!* But one thing I do know, I certainly wasn't expecting this.

"I don't drink coffee," I tell him, because I don't know what else to say.

He stops unwrapping his sandwich to smile at me, "I'll remember that for next time."

Next time?

I unwrap my sandwich and nearly groan in appreciation. *BLT! Yum!* I start eating it and drink the water that I already had. We sit there in silence for a few minutes, just eating, before I just have to ask him.

"What is this, Mr. Kane?"

"We're having lunch, Doc."

"I get that. What I don't understand is why."

"Why? Can't I just want to have lunch with you?"

"Mr. Kane, we discussed this. I can't and won't date…"

He reaches into the pocket of the leather vest he's wearing and pulls out a piece of paper, sliding it across the table to me.

"What's this?" I ask unfolding it. When I read it, my hand shakes. *What does he mean with this?*

"Three months clean, Doc. Me and my dick," he states, biting into his sandwich as if he's discussing the weather.

"I'm happy for you, Mr. Kane, but…"

"Relax, Doc. I wanted you to know that I'm not the man you first met, I've changed. Plus, I've thought on what you said, and I realized I've never had a woman friend."

"This news doesn't surprise me."

"Sarcasm can be ugly, Doc," he says with a wink.

I have to struggle not to choke on the water I'm swallowing.

"Anyways, I hate being called Mr. Kane, and I hate my first name. If I'm ever going to get you to call me Bull, I figure we need to be friends."

"Friends? Without benefits?" I clarify.

"Why Doc? Are you offering?"

"No. I mean, I just assumed that…I mean I don't want…."

He starts laughing, and I haven't heard him laugh before. It's a good sound. Solid and firm, warm and inviting and I should *not* be noticing it.

"Yeah, Doc. Just friends, no benefits, except you calling me Bull, and me spending time with you."

I ignore the sensation deep down inside of me that feels like disappointment at his offer. I give him my agreement with a smile. "Always happy to make new friends Mr…. I mean, Bull."

"That right there makes it all worth it."

"You'll have to explain that remark," I tell him drying my hands.

"Hearing you say my name with a smile on your face."

"And this, *all worth it?* What exactly does that mean?"

"You're a sharp one, Doc."

"Medical school and being a mom," I explain. "You can't afford to let a lot slip by you."

"Gotcha. Well that's a question for another day."

"It is?"

"Yeah. Tomorrow? Same place and time?" he asks.

"I don't work tomorrow."

"Then meet me for lunch."

"I'm sorry, I can't. I have plans." I tell him and wave at Buck and Alex, the cardiac floor nurse. Buck is one of the janitors on staff, I wasn't aware he and Alex were friends, but I like both of them, so it's nice to see.

"What kind of plans?" Bull persists, demanding my attention.

"Would a friend be asking me that?"

"Well, we're new friends, so allowances have to be made."

"That doesn't make a bit of sense. But, if you must know, I have a parent teacher conference tomorrow."

"Then meet me after it. Weavers? Come on. You haven't lived if you don't try one of their hotdogs."

I should say no. I almost have the words out, then I hear myself say, "Okay, around two?"

"Perfect," Bull says, and I don't know whether to kick myself or him for the cocky look of victory he's wearing.

AW

HER HAIR SHINES in the warm sun. When I look at her it's almost as if God is surrounding her with a halo. *An angel.* That's what she is. Always so kind and giving to everyone. I left her a note today in her locker telling her how much I loved her laugh. I saw the smile and the careful way she folded the note back up. I wanted to approach her then, but I stopped myself. I can't rush this. It has to be perfect. I must force myself to move slow and plan. I must be methodical. The last woman wasn't pure enough. She wasn't worthy. I have to make sure this time.

This time it must be perfect.

Chapter 4

BULL

I WATCH AS she walks towards me and my heart slams in my chest like I am some damn teenage boy. Skye is beautiful. She's curvy but athletic, her blue eyes sparkle, even from a distance, and that auburn hair adorns her head like a crown. I want to wrap my hands around it and feel it. Use it to hold onto her while she's sucking my cock, or, hell, when I bend her over a table and fuck her hard. Her skin is pale porcelain, and I can't help but imagine the pink hue it would turn after I spank her ass and the perfect outline of my hand that would be left behind. Jesus, I'm getting a hard-on in broad daylight standing outside of a fucking elementary school.

"Hi," she says, and she looks almost shy. Her cheeks are even tinted pink. That's not helping my poor dick at all. Now I want to know how deep that color can run. Will her whole body flush with color? Fuck are her nipples that same color?

"Hey, Doc. You look beautiful." It's not a lie, she's wearing a green sweater and blue jeans that cling to her perfectly, with these brown boots that click when she walks and mold to her legs. I've never found boots sexy, but on her they are. The green sweater brings out the gold, red, and other hues in her hair and hugs her generous breasts in a way that makes me jealous of it.

"I thought we were going to meet at Weavers?"

"It's just across the street. I saw you walk up about the time I got off my bike, figured I'd wait on you," I tell her. It's a lie. I was here early, because I wanted to see her with her son. Why? I do not know. I just know watching her with him, brought me pleasure. She's just how I thought she would be with him. Matty is a lucky boy.

We walk across the street and grab one of the outdoor tables.

"How did the meeting go?" I ask while we wait on service.

"Not bad. Matty's been having some trouble with some bullies at school. Being the new kid isn't the easiest thing in the world."

"How long have you lived here?" I ask. I could have had Freak find all this information out for me, but I didn't want to. I want to learn everything there is to know about Skye, but I just want her to be the one to give me the information.

"A little over six months. I wanted to do my residency here."

"In Kentucky? What on earth for?" I ask. I can't imagine a woman who invested the money and time it took for medical school to pick a small town in Kentucky to do her residency.

She laughs and the sound grabs a hold of my already hard dick, and I can feel him leak in my jeans. *Jesus.* I told her we'd be friends. What I didn't make clear is I was going to move straight from friends to lovers and move fucking fast. I spent three months getting my shit together. Each week that went by without seeing her, just made me want her more. I don't know that I truly believed in instant love. Dragon said the moment he saw Nicole he knew, even when he tried to fight it. I thought he was just thinking with his dick. Now, I admit I might have been wrong. Since I met Skye, no other woman has even been in the same ballpark.

"I wanted Matty to live in a small town away from all the demands and crowds of a big city like New York. It was important to me. I've made so many mistakes that Matty has had to deal with, I wanted to make sure I did everything I could to give him a good place to grow up."

"Mistakes? What kind?"

"Do friends really share that kind of information after only two lunch da...meetings?"

I grin, because I know she almost said date. *Oh, if she only knew my real plan for her.* I don't want her to run away. I can't let that happen.

"Tell you what Doc. How about we make up our own rules? I can pretty much guarantee and you probably already know this, but your mistakes can't be worse than mine. We can swap war stories and show off our battle scars."

"Battle scars?"

"We all have them, Doc. It's an army saying though."

She nods, but before she can talk the waitress comes in and takes our order. When I see her I almost panic. This might not have been such a great idea. I know that girl...Shit! *I've had my dick in—well on her.*

"Bull! I thought that was you! I haven't seen you at the last couple of club parties. Where have you been hiding?" she asks, bending down to hug me and nearly smothering me with her tits. I pull my head way back and angle away from her.

"I've been busy."

"What about tonight? I'm free if you'd like to meet up and have a little fun," she says, clearly not taking the hint.

"Devil's toenails," Skye mutters.

I look at her with a snort of laughter.

"Devil's toenails?" I ask, because I can't stop myself.

"I try not to curse so Matty doesn't pick up on it. You know how kids are."

I don't really, but something about that I *really* like.

"You have a kid?" The waitress says, and, for the life of me, I can't remember her name. She was some dumb chick I titty-fucked one night. It wasn't that great, but it got me off. That's about all that mattered.

"Yeah, a nine year old," Skye says. "Could I get a chicken salad and a bottle of water, please?"

"I don't want kids, at least until I'm older. Probably your age. I'm not ready to let my breasts get all saggy and shit. Not that yours are that bad," she says and I want to bang my head on the table because here's another example to Skye of what an idiot I've been.

"I'm sure. But then you won't need to worry about that. You may need to replace your silicone in a few years though."

"What? I'll have you know these are real."

"I'll have a foot-long hot dog with fries and a beer," I interject, even though Skye's comeback has me laughing. "Oh and make sure our order is handled by another server, or I'll tell Bill." The waitress shoots an evil look at both of us and stomps off.

"Who's Bill?" Skye asks.

"The owner."

"Ah. I see. Tell me, Bull. Am I to meet all of your play toys?"

"God, I hope not."

"I'm starting to think this was a bad idea."

"I warned you my mistakes would make yours pale in comparison."

"It would appear all of yours are of the female variety," she says. There's a hint of something in her voice that I'm praying is jealousy.

"You'd be surprised. But what does it matter? I mean we're just friends, right?"

She looks at me with that blush back in her cheeks, and, once again, my damn dick is pushing hard against the zipper of my jeans.

"Just friends," she agrees, and I have to bite my tongue.

Time, I just need time.

Chapter 5

SKYE

I SLAM THE door to the hospital security office. That was about as helpful as I thought it would be. I've been getting strange notes since about a month after I started work. Whoever is leaving them always manages to do it when no one is around. At least, no one remembers seeing them. It's driving me crazy. They're not bad notes, Judy jokes and tells me I have a secret admirer. I mostly laugh it off, but now they're coming more often. I've called the police about it, but since it has taken place only at work and nothing threatening is happening, they didn't seem inclined to worry about it. They told me to talk to hospital security about it. Security, in turn, said they would monitor the off duty rooms more. I'm pretty sure they just told me that to get rid of me.

I shrug it off and decide to think on something positive. I'm actually doing really well in my residency. Walter says I'm the leading candidate to work in the cardiac unit, which is what I've always wanted. His praise and promises of the future keep me from going crazy while I'm stuck doing ER rotation.

"I heard you've been dating Bull," Nurse Allen's voice hits me, and just like that my good thoughts are gone. I can't stand this woman. She and Dr. Eldridge are the huge dark spot that keeps me from enjoying my time here at this hospital. There are times I really wish I chose Corbin General for my residency. I picked London instead, because of the beautiful parks and small town feel. It has all that but still has restaurants and things that remind me of living in the city. It's the kind of place I've always wanted to raise a child in. The kind of place to make Matty happy. *I owe him that.* That leaves me trying to overlook these idiots. I manage most days. It looks like today is not one of those days.

"You heard wrong."

"Talk around our club is that you had lunch with him at Weavers."

"Your club? Do you have a secret password and everything?"

"Laugh it up all you want, but Bull is a member of the Savage Brothers. He's not going to be satisfied with a goody-two shoes like you. Bull's tastes run a little different. It takes a special kind of woman to keep him satisfied. Me and the other women of the club we know exactly what he likes."

The smirk on her face makes me sick. There's so much I really want to say, but I don't. It wouldn't do any good and I don't want to waste my time talking to her.

"I wouldn't know, Mr. Kane and I are just friends."

"Friends? I bet," she laughs scornfully.

"Yes, friends. You know that thing where a man and a woman talk with each other and don't do anything else, especially pass STD's back and forth," yeah, just like that I manage to not hold my mouth.

"You fucking bitch. I told you it wasn't me."

"Is there a problem here ladies?"

I look up to see Buck, leaning on his mop watching us. Melissa looks at him like he's dirt underneath her fingernails. God, I really hate that look. I've seen her give it to *too* many good people.

"Mind your own goddamn business. Don't you have some toilets to go scrub or something?" Melissa barks.

I will not slap her, I will not slap her. *God I want to slap her.* That's all I can think as Buck seems to ignore her and look at me with a friendly smile.

"You need anything, Skye?"

"No thanks, Buck. How are things? Did you finally purpose to that girlfriend of yours?"

"Not yet, I want to make sure everything is perfect. She's special."

"I don't suppose you have a brother?" I joke and ignore Melissa's sigh of disgust. When she finally leaves, I want to shout with glee.

"You better watch that one. I think she might have it out for you."

"I will. Thanks for saving me today," I tell him with a smile. I pat his arm, as I walk past him. "I better get going, my break was up five minutes ago."

"You have a good day," Buck, says and I wish him the same. I have to hurry to the nurse's station, so Alex can give me my next round of files.

Days like today make me wonder why I wanted to be a doctor in the first place. It sure did seem a lot more glamourous before medical school.

Chapter 6

SKYE

"ODD, BUT I thought friends *invited* friends over to their houses," I tell Bull when I open the door. This is the one-month anniversary of our friendship. Each week I've seen him at least twice and sometimes more. We usually eat lunch, or he will show up after I work a double shift and walk me to my car. I asked him how he seemed to know my schedule so well, and he just shrugged. I'm thinking I should start to call him stalker instead of friend, except I like having him around. Besides, the note I got in my locker today, says the stalker position has been filled. Today the note asked me if I liked roses. I wanted to scream no, and I hate notes from people I don't know.

Bull has been true to his word, and we've just been friends. I'm woman enough to admit that it bothers me that he seems to have accepted being my friend so easily. I mean, what woman wants a sexy man, to just accept being her friend without arguing about it? He's looking just as good right now, just like he always does. He is wearing his leather cut, and a baby blue t-shirt that looks well-worn and soft. I resist the urge to reach out and touch it. *Barely.*

"Aw, but friends show up to cheer up other friends unannounced."

I lean back against the doorframe and ask, even though I'm scared of what kind of answer he'll come up with. "And why do I need cheering up?"

"You told me Matty was going to Ohio for a school trip and then staying the night with a friend."

"Yeah?" I ask, not making a connection.

"Doc are you saying you don't miss your boy when he's not here? That you don't notice how quiet the house is? Or that you forget to eat because it's no fun eating by yourself?"

"You do realize this is a Friday night?"

"Yeah?"

"Shouldn't you be out, bopping some bimbo and making more mistakes, as you like to say?"

He steps closer—to the point that I can feel his breath on my skin, and I try not to react, that is no easy feat. The more time I spend with him, the more attracted I am.

"Doc, no one says bopping anymore. Hell, I'm not sure they ever did say bopping."

"They do when they have a nine year old in the house."

"Whatever. I keep telling you I'm a reformed man. Maybe someday you'll believe it. Are you going to invite me in?"

"Will you leave if I don't?"

"Do you want me to?"

I sigh, defeated. This is a familiar game, and I'm pretty sure he has me figured out.

"Come on in. I was just getting ready to order a pizza."

"Already done, the delivery guy should be here any time."

"Umm…you don't know what I like on pizza."

He shrugs, "I ordered one with cheese and one with every-thing. I figure you could pick off what you don't want, or eat the plain cheese one.

"You do know you're crazy," I tell him, because at this

point I'm at a loss.

"No. I just saw something I wanted a little over four months ago, and I'm working towards that goal. Besides, I wanted to talk with you."

At first his words don't click and then they *do*. It feels like I'm sucker punched. I don't know what to say for a minute. *Maybe I misunderstood him?*

"Something you wanted? I thought we were going for friendship?"

"And we have, Doc. But eventually, I'm going to ask for more from you and when I do, you'll give it to me."

His words alternate between pissing me off and scaring the hell out of me.

"I think you should go."

"No."

"What?"

"I'm not leaving. We're going to sit down and watch a movie, eat some pizza and then make out a little. Isn't that what you do on dates?"

"We're not dating!" I growl at him. Terrified now, because I *really* want to make out with him.

"Doc. C'mon now. We've had lunch too many times to count. I see you practically every evening you work late. I'm pretty sure that qualifies as dating, even if I haven't done it before."

"I can't date you!"

"Why the fuck not?"

"You're a man-whore!"

"Again. Let's repeat it together. A *reformed* one. I'll have you know my dick has been nowhere since the moment I saw you. Well except my hand. But hey, even then it was with visions of you in my head."

He says it so casually. Like what he said didn't just rock my world. He's leaning on the doorframe and looking so calm and collected and inside I'm scared to death.

"You could have HIV or anything! You've slept with the sluttiest nurse since the invention of porn movies!"

"Mistakes. But all in the past. You have my test results. Here's the latest batch. You've changed me, Doc," he says pulling out a folded paper from his pants pocket, but I don't have to look. He's been showing me each month. I thought it was to show me how much better he's doing…Now, I can see it was for other reasons. I'm just not sure how I feel about it.

"Are you making fun of me? Do you think this is a joke?"

That must have pissed him off, because suddenly the look of ease he normally wears is gone and in its place is anger. You can feel in vibrating between us.

"No it's not a fucking joke, Doc. What's a fucking joke is the woman I'm attracted to, the woman who manages to haunt my damn dreams at night—freaks out at the thought of going on a date with me!"

"You said we were friends!"

"Friends turn into lovers!"

I back away from him. I'm reacting wildly, I know. The thing is, he's offering something I want, but have told myself I can't have. Bull is a mistake that would be too big to recover from. *He's not safe.* He's the complete *opposite* of safe. I took that leap once before and it left me knocked up and totally alone. I need to be smarter now. *Matty needs me to be smarter.*

"I have a kid, Bull. I can't just decide to date someone like you."

"Someone like me?" he asks, his voice cold.

"You have sex like other people change their clothes. A different woman every day, and you admitted sometimes two or three times a day."

"Not since…"

"Maybe not since me, if I trust what you say. I'm not sure I can trust you though."

"Damn it, Skye…"

"*But even then*," I carry on, interrupting him. "Even then, Bull, you had so many different drugs in your system. How could I ever let someone like that around my child? Not to mention you exposed yourself to HIV and AIDS and it can take three to six months for that stuff to show up. How could I let you in my bed, knowing I have a child who depends on me? I'm all he has, Bull. Even if I wanted to be crazy and throw caution to the wind, I can't. I have to think of Matty, first."

He steps back from me, and there's a look that comes over his face. He doesn't say anything, but I can see he's deep in thought. There's part of me scared. I've come to depend on Bull this last month. Which is crazy, because we have just been friends. What happens if he leaves and doesn't come back? The thought of not seeing him every day or having at least some contact with him frightens me.

"We could still be friends, Bull," I offer because I don't want to let him go, even if I should.

"Woman. *I don't want to be just your friend.* You haunt me. I can't sleep at night. I have fucking callouses on my hand, because the minute my eyes close I see your face. My goddamn dick gets so fucking hard, I have to stroke it over and over, imagining it's you jacking me, begging for my cum. And when I come, Skye? It's always to the vision of coming all over your fucking body, while you beg for more. But hell, even in my sleep you still haunt me. I dream of fucking you over and over—only to wake up needing you again."

"Bull…" I back up as his words brand me. My stomach

flutters. I look into this dark eyes and see the way he's watching me fills me with heat. "You said we were going to be friends…"

He closes the small distance between us. His hand slides under my hair as he cups the back of my neck. His thumb brushes the side of my face, before stopping beside the lobe of my ear and applying pressure, so I can't move.

"Do you think of me, Doc? When you're in bed alone, do you wonder what I'm doing? Do you want to hear my voice? When I call to tell you goodnight and we hang up, do you find your hand sliding down between your legs? Do you touch yourself and imagine it's my touch making you come? Do you cry out my name when you climax?"

His words make my knees weak. I feel my face heat, because *I do*. I do all of those, even knowing I shouldn't. I do them, thinking no one will ever know, and yet he somehow does.

"Bull, we're too different," That's what I keep telling myself, though in truth, the more time I spend with him, the less I believe it.

"I've been clean for four months now, Doc. I've proved what you thought of me is wrong. I'm going to keep proving you wrong—on every count. What I'm wondering is what you'll come up with after that to stop this?"

"This?"

"You and me, Doc. Because you need to fucking set your mind to it. We're happening. *You and me.* And you need to mark it down, because we're going to be kissing, making out, and fucking. It's *going* to happen and you will enjoy every damn minute of it," he growls at me.

Then it happens. That moment I'll never get back, but will always remember. His mouth slams down on mine. It's an angry kiss and I do my best to keep my lips closed, until he sucks the bottom one into his mouth. His tongue teases and tempts to the point I can't stop my gasp, needing oxygen. He swallows the sound, his tongue forcefully moves in my mouth, and then he devours me. His kiss is unlike any I've ever had before. He not only explores, he *owns*. I can do nothing but follow his lead, and our tongues twist and mate, tasting each other. I strain into him, pulling him down to me, even more— afraid he will leave. I never want the kiss to end. A shudder rakes through my body and I can't help the restless way I move against him, as moisture pools between my thighs. *I need him.* All the pent up attraction I've kept hidden the last month is dying to be unleashed. His kiss manages to excite me in a way that no foreplay has ever managed previously. Before I explore it though, Bull pulls away.

"You said it would be six months before you could trust my test results."

My mind is foggy and I have no idea what he's talking about, "What?" I ask, trying to stop the way my body trembles with need.

"Six months. It's been four. I'm going to give you two more months to get used to this, Skye. But I'm not backing down from us. I am kissing you and spending time with you. You need to get used to it and wrap your mind around the idea that you and I are going to happen."

I don't say anything, because I'm not sure what to say. The doorbell rings and neither of us move for a second. Then, he kisses my forehead, wraps his hands around my upper arms and just holds me like that.

"Get us some drinks. I'll pay for the pizza and we'll watch a movie."

"But…"

"For now we'll cuddle and watch television, Skye. I'm not asking for anything else."

"Oh…okay," I answer. I'm lost. I'm so confused, I don't know what I want or feel.

"Tonight at least," he tags on ominously, and my brain refuses to think about that.

I'm going to be Scarlet O'Hara for now, and think about it all tomorrow.

Chapter 7

SKYE

I LOOK AT the note on my locker. *Another damned note.* Not threatening, or even scary—but they are getting irritating.

You look nice today—Always Watching

That's how he always signs it. Always Watching. If anything that's the part that's creepy. I wad it up with a sigh.

"Secret admirer again?" Judy asks, she's a resident too, and she and I have become pretty good friends.

"I guess. He must be trying to up his game. This is the second note I've had this month."

"I still think you should report it to the police."

"I tried once, they pretty much laughed me off. I've report-ed it to hospital security. What could I tell the police now? That I'm getting more notes bragging on the way I look? If anything else happens maybe. It's nothing. Heck, it's probably just someone trying to scare the new girl," I tell her, dismissing it all.

"Or some perv whacking off to you every night."

"Eww… that's too gross to even think about Judy."

"Hey people are fucked up."

"Well, if he does anything else besides write me more notes, I'll worry about it then."

"Yeah, I guess there's not much to worry about with weird notes. He can't be bad, or he'd be jealous of that hot hunk of man-meat you've been eating lunch with."

"Bull and I are just friends," I lie. Hell, I'm not sure what we are. We kiss. We have lunch or dinner. We've even met at the movies once. It's never went beyond handholding and kissing. Bull says he's giving me time to accept things, until he get his all clear for six months. Then, he says all bets are off. That's not that far away. I have no idea what to do, and time is quickly running out.

"Then girl you are insane. If I had that man sniffing around me, I'd push him up against the wall, climb him like a damn tree, wrap my legs around his neck, and introduce him to the original southern comfort. Hell, I'd keep him there until I died or he was smothered to death."

I laugh, while tossing the note into the back of my locker. Her words make me picture doing exactly that to Bull. If I'm honest, my hormones are going crazy for this man, and I'm weakening with each hot look he gives me. I'm just...*scared*. That's what it all boils down to. I pull my phone from the locker to listen to my messages. If anything urgent happens with Matty the school always calls the hospital and has me paged, but I still worry. So, I don't like to leave them un-checked.

I smile when I see the text from, Bull.

Can't do lunch today, Doc. Club business. I'll call you later. Miss you, beautiful.

P.S. Three more days.

I can't stop the goofy smile and I'm so engrossed in think-ing about him, that I don't notice Judy reading over my shoulder.

"Damn, Skye! Remind me again why you haven't tied him to your bed?"

"I'm starting to wonder that myself," I whisper.

"If you girls are done gossiping in here, there are patients out there who could use our attention."

I look up at Dr. Eldridge standing in the doorway. The man is such a douche bag. I can barely stomach him. Had I known he'd be the chief attending physician, I would have never ended up here in London. When I think of Bull, I know that would have been a mistake. I don't know what our friendship is, but I know that I wouldn't want to miss it.

Judy and I don't respond, instead we slam our lockers shut and go around Dr. Eldridge without comment. We are walking down the hall towards the nurse's station when Judy whispers, "Fuck girl, I think he's gotten more hateful since he stopped screwing that ho-bag Melissa. I wish someone would step up and take one for the team."

"*Ew.* I don't know anyone that desperate."

"Especially after Melissa told everyone about his pencil dick."

"Eh, she'll find a way to weasel back up to him soon, and then maybe we can get a breather."

"One could hope. By the way, what's so special about three more days?"

"You're nosy."

"It's a gift."

I laugh, and then take a deep breath. "We haven't had sex."

"*What?*" She yells out and I wince and feel my face flush. All the nurses and other staff are looking at us. I hiss at her—feeling my face blush as Alex and some of my other friends look at me. I'm afraid they know exactly what we're talking about. *I want to kill Judy.*

"Will you keep it down? I told you how we met and who he had been doing the mattress mambo with!"

"Damn girl, everyone has a past. No one says you have to marry the guy, but don't go passing up a little fun."

"Yeah well, the clap is a big price to pay for a little fun."

"You're a doctor. You know safety is our friend. Shit, girl. Go get an itch scratched. Fuck. Scratch one or two for me."

"Like you have any. You have Tony."

"Yeah, and I love him, but marriage kills sex. I swear I've been thinking about calling a code blue on his dick and seeing if the paddles will bring it back to life."

I laugh so hard, I literally snort. "Like I believe that. You have four kids, Judy. That doesn't just happen by divine intervention."

"Yeah, but the youngest will be one next week, and since then it's been as dry as the Sahara Desert. Hell, I think knocking me up this last time, broke him."

"Maybe it's time you climbed him like a tree and offered him some southern comfort."

"Maybe, but I got a feeling your man would be a lot wilder ride."

I know he would be, and maybe that's what scares me.

What if I don't survive the ride?

AW

I DON'T THINK she even noticed me today. She was too engrossed in talking about that Neanderthal biker. I knew if she kept hanging out with him, there would be trouble. That other doctor, with the brown hair, she's filling Skye's mind with impure thoughts. I may have to do something to keep her away until I'm ready to start Skye's training.

Accidents happen so easily. Especially to women who have no morality.

It's definitely time for Judy Greene to learn that.

Past time.

Chapter 8

BULL

MADE SKYE a promise to give her time so she would know I was serious. To go slow—to go day-by-day. That seems to be how I live my life these days. It's something this support group that Dani hooked me up with has taught me. I look at the round medallion I got tonight. *Six months clean.* It doesn't sound like much. In the grand scheme of things, it's probably not. Still, it means a hell of a lot to me. It's a milestone. I'm slowly getting my life back together. It didn't take long to fall into the gutter and maybe I wasn't there long, but it felt like a lifetime.

Losing Red to Dancer was a fool's game. I knew as I was falling for her that she was in love with him. I just couldn't help myself. I was drawn to her. Like a moth to a motherfucking flame, the heat and the color catches your eye and even though you know it's bad for you, you keep going towards it—unable to stop. Hell, I'm not sure I was in love with her. She represented something I wanted, something I'd never had. An innocence that shown even in the darkness that surrounded me. I grieved her loss, even though I didn't have a right.

I came close to dying and even that didn't bother me. The fact that I let Red down, the fact that Dancer had to save her, and that he and Drag also saved my sorry ass, *that* hit me. It hit me down into my gut and set up a poison there that ate at me. I'm the club enforcer. The strong arm that is supposed to make sure shit like that doesn't happen, and I got my ass handed to me while I was lying in bed drunk, dreaming about another man's woman.

It's stupid, but I know that was the beginning. The beginning of my fall into hell.

In my mind, I deserve the migraines I'm plagued with and the tremors I get in my hands. They are my punishment for being the weak asshole that let down his family, just when they needed him most. The pain is bad. There are nights I can barely function from the headaches, but they don't outweigh the bitterness in my gut.

Then Jay, a buddy from service had his sister contact me. *Cancer.* He was dying and there wasn't a damn thing I could do about it. He needed me and I let him down. All the fucking shit with Nicole and Dani went down. Hell, Nicole got kidnapped while I was on the phone with my buddy begging me to come to him. I felt guilt tearing at me through both ends, but in the end I chose my club over Jay. Dragon pulled his fucking stunt and Jay died before I could even get there to see him. He became yet another person I let down. Just like I let Red and the club down, just like I let Nicole down. My failures kept piling up, one right after the other.

I fell a little deeper.

The thing about falling into hell is that the fall is quick. The fall happens before you even fucking realize it. You wake up one morning, popping pills to avoid the pain, to numb the guilt. You've given your dick to a bitch you should have never touched, in exchange for a fix, and you can hear the devil laugh. He's laughing because he knows and you know that you're in so deep you'll never find your way out.

Except, I did.

I pinch the medallion between my thumb and forefinger. *Six months.* The brothers have no idea. That was on purpose. They already knew I had been fucking up. Hell, Dragon bypassed me completely when he should have depended on me the most. I understand why he did it, it doesn't mean it didn't hurt like a motherfucker and help push me a little further down. In his shoes, I'd have done the same fucking thing. *Still.* In *my* shoes, it was just another sign that I had failed so many times even my brothers, my family, didn't trust me.

All that leads to now. Standing outside the local community center, holding a medallion that to me is a big accomplishment, with not one person to share it with—well Dani, but all I could do was text her and have her congratulate me. She's been a rock, though. Letting me pour my heart out over the phone and not judging me, even when I'm craving a fix. She gets it. Hell, she even lets me go on and on about Skye.

Skye. We've been taking it slow. A few kisses and holding hands, Jesus, I'm like a regular boyfriend, and my dick hates me for it.

I text or call her every day, and most days we at least have lunch together. I haven't seen her at all this week though. She knows some of what I'm doing, and I think she's scared. No, I *know* she's scared, but she is also cheering me on. At least from a distance—that was on purpose. I need to give her time to prepare, because I had Poncho from the club run some more tests today. The minute those come back tomorrow, all bets are off. She'll be out of excuses, and I'm not allowing her to think of more.

I pick up my phone, punch in the numbers and wait.

"Hello?"

Her voice soothes every nerve ending I have and brings me

more peace than I probably have a right to feel.

"Hey, Doc," my voice sounds hoarse and raw and I clear it. Too many memories are surrounding me tonight. Too many wounds are uncovered, but I couldn't not call her.

"Hey, Bull," her soft, warm voice comes back at me and I picture her sitting on the sofa curled up in that ugly ass afghan she keeps on the back of her couch, drinking hot chocolate and reading. I know that's most likely what she was doing before I called. "How did it go?" she asks, because she knows what tonight was and where I've been.

"Six months down, got the medallion to prove it."

"That's good. I'm proud of you. I would have been there if you let me, you know."

She would have. I do know that. Not like I want her to be though. She's offered her friendship over and over. That's not what I want. Well, it's not *all* I want. I want all of her. Every last damn bit and I haven't pushed her this last month (*well not too hard*), because she was right in some ways. However, now that I am seeing daylight, now that I'm climbing out, and know I can leave it all behind, I'm tired of waiting.

"I know."

"Bull…"

"I don't want to fight, Doc. Not tonight. I told you where this is going. I wasn't lying."

She sighs, but she doesn't argue. It wouldn't do her any good if she did.

"You're a stubborn man," she says finally.

"Why do you think they call me, Bull?" I joke. "What are you doing?"

"Just got Matty down, getting ready to crash."

"I'll let you get back to it. I'll see you soon."

"Bull, we really should talk about…"

"I'll see you soon, Doc and then you'll be out of excuses," I warn her as I hang up the phone. I'm not joking. Once I have my test results back…

All bets are off.

Chapter 9

SKYE

"HEY ALEX? DO you know where Judy is today?" I ask as I return the charts from my rounds. I missed Judy and I need her to calm me down about what's going on with Bull. Plus, she always keeps me laughing and manages to make the day go faster.

"You didn't hear?"

"Hear what?"

"Her house caught on fire last night."

"What? Oh no! Is everyone okay?"

"Yeah, but the back door was jammed and Judy almost died. Luckily Tony came home in time to get her out. Her children were with him."

"Well that's good."

"Yeah. She turned in some leave. They're going to move in with her parents in Somerset while they regroup."

"God I hate that. If you find out her contact information there, or if everyone takes up a donation for her, will you let me know?"

"Sure thing."

"Thanks, Alex. I guess I better get back to it. I'm working a double and they tell me that tonight is a full moon."

"Damn."

"Exactly," I laugh and head back to work, wishing I could talk to Judy now. I'll try her cell at break.

I spend the rest of the day on auto pilot. I had to deal with Dr. Eldridge and Nurse Allen a few times and I literally had to bite the inside of my jaw to keep from going off on them. I need to talk to Walter. I hate to try and pull the old, my-connections-are-bigger-and-better-than-yours card, but I'm getting desperate. I grab another chart and head into the exam room.

"Hey Doc."

"Bull…" I say, my body laced with shock. He looks so good. Jesus, I've missed seeing him this week. It feels like it's been forever. We've been exchanging short phone calls and texts, but that's it.

"Wasn't expecting to see me?" he asks all cocky, already knowing the answer.

"Do I dare ask what you're doing here?" I try not to show him my smile. I shouldn't feel like smiling—*but I do.* Inside there's a little girl in me shouting; *He's here! He's here!*

I've had a bad night. I hate working the graveyard shift and not only because it leaves Matty with my neighbors. Tonight is extra bad. People laugh but there is something about a full moon that always calls the crazies in. From the patients, the staff being extra stressed, to finding two new notes from my stalker. I've been here twenty-four hours straight and I'm dragging ass. It's all I can do to pick one foot up in front of the other. Then, I walk in and find Bull here and bam, I feel energized.

I look at him over my chart, trying to hide behind it. He looks as mouthwatering as usual. Dark skin, long sleeved thermal red shirt worn under his cut and the earring in his right ear shines in the florescent office lighting above us. His strong, hard face has a hint of playfulness in it, and his black velvety eyes glow. He's so broad and muscular, he makes me feel small. It's not that I'm huge by any stretch of the imagination, but a woman who is a size fourteen and stands five foot ten hardly ever gets the chance to feel small.

"I'm having chest pains," he says, and that catches my attention. I look through his chart, but I can't find a record of anything in his past history. It worries me, because sometimes stopping medication, no matter how long you've been abusing it, can be rough on your heart.

"How long has this been going on?" I ask him, opening up the correct page in his chart to take notes.

"For about six months now," he answers, his voice serious.

"You haven't mentioned it before. Bull, you should have told me. We should have been monitoring you. Have you had any other symptoms that you might not have noticed?"

"Like what?" He asks.

I warm my stethoscope in my hand by cupping it, and then push the collar of his shirt down so that I can place it against his chest and listen to his heart. I try to still my pulse rate, and my reaction to being this close to him. It's not easy. The sound of his heartbeat fills my ears. It's strong and steady—if not a little quick. The beat of it causes me to react and I feel myself getting wet. *At my place of work. Where I should be my most professional.* I look up and find my eyes trapped by his.

"What do you hear, Doc?" He says and I can't help but watch the soft movement of his lips as they form words. The fullness of them, the moisture over the dark skin, the glimpse at his white teeth and, being able to see just the tip of his tongue. How have I not noticed how sexy a man's lips could be before? *Dang it!*

I clear my throat and ignore his question. I'm pretty sure I hear my ovaries crying out, *please*. I go through the motions with the rest of the physical exam. I listen to his lungs, then check his ears and eyes. It's all repetitive stuff, but right now, nothing about it feels routine.

I sit down to make my notes. "Has there been any other symptoms that you can think of?"

"Like what?" He asks, reclining back against the hospital exam bed. Again, I make it my job to ignore the way his thermal shirt stretches over his muscles.

"Nervousness? Lethargy? Trouble sleeping? Depression? You'd be surprised of all the strange symptoms of heart problems.

"I've been really horny lately," he answers and I accidentally drop the chart on the ground. It's then that I know, yet again, he's playing games. I should have expected it of course. It's just when he mentioned chest pains, I immediately went into doctor mode. He scared me and made me go through all of this. *For nothing.*

"Bull, I should have expected this. You had me worried, you donkey butt! You need to leave, there are legitimate patients outside in the waiting room that require *real* medical attention," I huff, standing up.

"I've missed your made up words. Did you really want to call me Jackass, Doc?"

"You need to leave. I don't have time for this. You don't get to come in here, taking up my time to make fun of me.

"You've got me all wrong, Doc. I do require real medical attention. My chest literally hurts when I think of how long I've gone without a woman."

"Christ's toenails! Are you for real? Do you even appreciate the fact that while you're in here trying to get laid, outside there are sick children and older adults, who need medical care?

You're preventing that from happening!

"Did you just say, Christ's toenails? Is that even a make-believe curse word?"

I ignore him, turning to leave the room. Bull grabs my arm, and keeps me from escaping. I look over my shoulder at him and luckily his mouth is nowhere near as tempting this time. That is, until he maneuvers my hand to his cock. Even through his pants I can tell he's rock hard. The heat is coming off of him in waves and seeps into my body. I fight the urge to wrap my hand around the solid outline of his dick. His pants are loose and worn enough, it'd be so easy to grasp him and hold him...*just once.*

Instead I yank my arm, trying to pull away. His strong hand, encircles my wrist, refusing to let me.

"Bull."

"Doc, you're killing me. I've been hard as a steel spike since the night we met, and it's not getting any better. My boys are turning fucking blue. Be honest, you've missed me this week. Let me hear you say it."

"No one said you had to go this long without sex," I tell him, hating the words even as I say them. The thought of him with someone else bothers me, and makes me literally sick to my stomach.

"I don't want anyone but you. Hell, I can't even get hard for anyone else. If I wear protection will you finally let me between your legs, Doc? Hell, I'll even double bag it."

"You shouldn't wear two condoms at once. It can increase the friction and..."

"Trust me, Doc. There'd be plenty of friction."

"...and the condom would more than likely rip or tear," I continue, ignoring him.

"Doc. Come on. Let's stop playing this game. You want

me as much as I want you. You might be pretending to be unaffected, but I bet if I checked right now your panties would be wet."

"Dr. Walker! What on earth are you doing?"

I jerk my hand away quickly from Bull. Or at least I try, Bull *still* refuses to let me. So here I am, holding Bull's impressive package, in front of my boss—and not just any boss.

No. The man standing in front of me is Dr. Reynolds. *My Chief of Staff.*

Chapter 10

BULL

I WATCH THE color bleed from Skye's face, and then turn my attention away from her to look at the man who just came in. He's older. Probably early forties, his hair is graying on the edges. His eyes are glued on Skye and for a second I see something I don't like. *Interest.* I pull her hand away from my dick and bring it up to my lips to kiss it. The man's eyes follow the movement and hate flashes in his eyes. *Fuck you, motherfucker. You're not getting her.*

"Dr. Reynolds, it's not what it looks like," Skye starts to explain, and I can't help but smile.

"It looks like you're inappropriately handling a patient…"

"Actually, I'm her man," I interject, going to stand in front of the doctor.

"Her man?" he asks, over the sound of Skye's sputtering.

That look on his face returns again, and right there I push forward. I pull Skye into me, my arm tight on her shoulder. She's stiff, but even with that, she feels amazing. I shouldn't have just showed up today. I should have called her, or arranged a time with her to meet tomorrow, after she rested. *I just couldn't not see her.* Watching the way this asshole is eyeing her, makes me think I should have been here much sooner.

"Yeah, me and Doc have been dating for the last six

months," I tell him and I know he can see the ownership stamped in my eyes. He better take fucking heed to it and stay away from her.

"I wasn't aware of that," he says, as he looks between me and Skye. For some reason his entire attitude is pissing me off.

"Why would you?"

"Well I am Skye's boss, as well as her friend."

I look over my shoulder at Skye. She seems frozen and unsure of what to say. I get the feeling I'm missing a very important piece to the puzzle, but I'll find it out later. It's time I put this asshole in his place.

"Yeah, me and sugar-tits here have been keeping it quiet. We didn't really want to put it out there until we knew for sure it was going to work. You know Doc, she likes to move slowly."

I hear Skye gasp behind me. I'm probably going to pay for that sugar-tits remark. I can't find a reason to care. She should be proud I haven't decked this guy yet.

"Well, she would because of Matthew."

The fact that he knows about Doc's son pisses me off. If it was just because he works with her, that'd be one thing. But, it's as clear as the nose on his face that he wants my woman. That's a problem, because she's mine.

"Walter, I was just…"

Walter's phone rings, interrupting her, and I'm damn glad.

"One minute, Skye," he says holding his hand up. He steps away from us to take his call, and that better be the last fucking time he uses her first name.

Skye tugs, trying to get away from me. "Sugar-tits?"

"God's honest truth, Doc, I wake up hard thinking about how sweet they will taste or feel wrapped around my cock."

"Will you keep your voice down? Oh my God! What are

you doing? Why are you letting my boss think we are a couple? Are you certifiably insane?" she whispers in anger. Her face is red, not quite as red as her hair, but damn cute.

Skye is a gorgeous woman. I'm man enough to admit that was her draw at first. She's tall and curvy and has the kind of legs a man wants wrapped around him all night long. Her sparkling blue eyes with flecks of gold in them, have haunted my dreams over the last few months. Her hair is a deep auburn red with hints of sunshine running through it. And her tits...large enough a man could bury his dick between and fuck them hard. Just the thought makes my already hard cock jerk and beg in reaction.

"Bull!" she huffs. "Let me go!" she demands when I don't answer her.

"We are a couple, right? Or have you been talking to any other motherfucker every day and eating lunch with them or kissing them goodnight?"

"What? Well no, but we haven't actually..."

"Would you rather I tell your boss how you've stepped over the edge of professional courtesy since day one? How he saw you playing with my dick and if he had been ten more minutes he would have seen you gagging on my cock, because you love sucking me? I know because you've done it numerous times, right here in this very exam room."

"What? I haven't!"

"He won't know that, will he? After what he just saw, I figure he'd believe me over you."

"You wouldn't dare!"

She's spitting fire at me and I should feel at least a little bit guilty. I don't. I'm enjoying this, like I haven't enjoyed anything in forever. Skye makes me feel alive again.

"Try me, sugar-tits," I tell her using the nickname she

hates. "Wouldn't it be better for him to think we're dating, or that you've been using me for sex, while patients sit out there needing medical treatment?"

"Who are you?"

"The man you've drove to the point of madness. And while we're on the subject, I'm also the man who's not about to let Walter-boy think he has a fucking shot with you. I told you Skye. We are happening. It's better he knows now, before I have to beat the hell out of him. Which I will still do, if he doesn't stop looking at your tits like he has been."

"Oh my God! I think I hate you now!"

"Is that anyway to treat the love of your life? Now smile, Walter-boy is coming back over here," I tell her, pulling her back to me and squeezing her ass.

"I'll kill you for this," she growls.

"Sure, right after you explain why your boss seems to think he has a shot with you."

"What?" she stutters, and I was right. Oh Walter-boy has been putting the moves on my woman. Good thing I got here today. "Smile, it's show time, lover," I whisper.

"That was Dr. Hoffensinger. The emergency bioprosethic valve replacement surgery is a go. I had thought it would be something you'd like to scrub in on, but of course if your attention is diverted, I can find…"

"No! No, I want to be there, Walter. You know how important this is to me," Skye speaks up and the way she keeps calling him *Walter* annoys the fuck out of me.

"Very well, if you want, you can walk with me," he answers, looking between us, and I don't think it's my imagination when I notice the way he's looking at me—as if he has won a battle. He might have, but I don't think *Walter* realizes, just what kind of war I can wage.

"Definitely," she says and pulls away from me. That annoys me too, but I don't let her go. I let her walk until the grip I have on her hand pulls her back. She looks over her shoulder, as if she just remembers I'm standing here. That *definitely* pisses me off.

"Bull, I need to…"

I jerk her back so that she stops mid-sentence. She falls onto my chest. Her hands brace against me and I like the way her nails bite into my skin. I put my fingers under her chin and bring her face up to mine. Her warm breath stutters over my chin and neck. Awareness runs through my body. Why does she feel so perfect in my arms?

"You forgot to kiss me goodbye, Doc. That can't be allowed," I warn her and then my lips find hers. I drink from her, my tongue seeking hers out. It takes some coaxing but when my hand cups her breast, her tongue starts sliding against mine, dancing against it. The kiss deepens, and I swallow the moan she gives when my thumb brushes against her plump nipple. I can tell, even through her clothes and lab coat, that her nipples are big. Fuck, I'd love to have them in my mouth to tease and torture….

"Really! Doctor Walker!"

Fucking, Walter. I'm going to have to do something to take care of that fool. Skye's body goes rigid and she pulls away from me. Her eyes seek mine out, hers are full of confusion, but her lips are swollen and well kissed. *By me.* Which is what I wanted.

She doesn't say anything, instead she follows Walter-boy out. When she gets to the door she looks back at me. I don't know what it means, but when she licks her lips, I figure it can't be all bad.

AW

SHE TOUCHED HIM! I don't like that at all. I thought getting her away from Judy would help, but apparently I was wrong. Instead, Skye acts upon the carnal thoughts Judy put in her mind. He's pushing her into something she doesn't want. I can see it in her eyes, but if she doesn't start staying him away I will have to act.

I'm not ready. Things like this can't be rushed. It looks like I will have to bring Skye down to the bottom so I can be the one to console her. She needs to learn it is me that she can turn to. She must learn that I am her salvation, her master.

It makes me sad that it must be this way. Why does she make it more painful? Does she crave it? That's something to consider. I will watch her a little longer to see exactly what path I must take. I have to be careful. I don't want this to end wrong like the last time.

This time it must be different. Skye must be forever.

Chapter 11

SKYE

I HAVE A problem, and it's a very *big* problem. I don't know what the hell is wrong with me. I should be telling Bull exactly where to go, not going along with this stupid game. Walter would be pissed, but he'd get over it. I don't think he would fire me, I'm pretty sure he'd believe me. Except I've already had two bad reports against me from Dr. Eldridge and Nurse Allen. Walter is the reason I've not really felt the heat from those. I know it's because he wants more than friendship with me. He's become more and more insistent about that the last month. The sane thing to do would be to extricate myself from all of it. What's the worst that could happen? So, maybe I'd have to go to another hospital to finish my residency. Would that really be so bad? I wanted London because I needed a town that was less stressful and busy. I needed a place where both Matty and I could be happy. London seemed like the answer to a prayer. Now, I'm not so sure.

Walter has been bad-tempered with me since we left Bull. In truth, he spoke down to me in the operating room. The other nurses and doctors were giving me strange looks, I know they picked up on it. I should have walked out, but I wanted to be there. I hope to specialize in cardiothoracic surgery. I have three more years of general surgical residency and then I can actually spend my time learning the heart full time. In the meantime, I live for moments like the ones just thrown in my lap. I can't just give them up. When I hold a heart in my hand and gently coax it back to beating, it's a feeling I can't describe.

I take off my surgery covering and toss them in the bin. It's beyond my break time and after the bitchiness of the last two hours, I need some air.

"Dr. Walker, we should talk about what happened earlier," I look around to see Walter standing by the door that leads into the operating room.

"It's nothing. Trust me, it won't happen again."

He wants to talk further, I can see it in his expression, but the rest of the OR staff starts filing out, and I get to escape. I stop by my locker to shed my damn lab coat. I'm done for the night. I just need to get my head straight so I can drive home to Matty. I freeze when I see the note. This wasn't what I needed tonight.

You're too pure to be defiled—AW

What the hell does that mean? I wad it up in my hand. I should be glad I guess. Maybe that means rape isn't on the weirdo's radar. Maybe I should report it to the police? I make a note to go by hospital security again tomorrow.

Right now, I just need out of here. I start walking, and I don't stop until I reach the door to the stairs. I'm taking big gulping breaths by the time I'm out on the roof. I bend over, grab my knees sucking air in, and try to slow my heartbeat.

How did I get here in my life? So many mistakes are behind me, the road is littered with them. That's the real reason I'm terrified of Bull. I wasn't lying. I can't afford more mistakes, and Bull has the potential to be the one mistake I can't recover from.

Thinking about my past always leads me back to the one thing in my life that altered my future and continues to do so. Matty means everything to me. I never meant to get pregnant at sixteen. It was one stupid night in the bed of an old Ford truck. Luke was the local football stud, and the most popular guy in the entire school. I thought I was lucky to have him look twice at me. We dated for a month and I thought we were in love. When he took me out to the top of the mountain where kids went to party, I knew what it meant. He had thrown an old mattress in the back of the truck and we laid on it and talked for hours, gazing up at the stars. I thought I was ready for what came next. A failed rubber, a jock who later told me he had a hundred dollars riding on whether or not he could *'bust my cherry'*, and parents who disowned me, told me I wasn't ready—*not at all.* Not even a little bit.

I walk over to the edge of the roof to look out over the evening sky and lights below. The sun is just starting to set, and the lights from the parking lot and businesses surrounding the hospital are coming on, one at a time. This is my favorite time of the day and the scene below calms me. I need to call Blair, my neighbor, to check on Matty and tell him I'll be home to tuck him in. It's been hard putting myself through medical school and now doing my residency with a young child. My late hours since starting my residency have definitely been the hardest part. I couldn't do it without Blair and her husband David. They're lifesavers, but I hate that I'm not there for Matty, like I need to be.

I turn away from the view. I need to walk back to my locker and get my phone. Just as I'm about to, Bull comes through the door. We stare at each other for what seems like forever. I don't want to see him. Not here, not right now, and definitely not with my emotions still raw from the memory of our kiss.

"Hey, Doc," he says, looking at me as if he has all of life's mysteries solved. I think I could hate him a little at this moment. He's managed to sneak past my defenses, and I can't seem to push him back out. He gets to me like a man hasn't in a long time. Hell, I'm lying. I doubt *any* man has *ever* gotten to me like he does. There hasn't been a lot of room for men in my life. Still, what he pulled today and the mess it's made with Walter is huge.

Walter has been at me for months to go out with him. I have put him off, telling him Matty has to be my number one priority, and there's just no time for anything left over. I know he's going to ask me why I've been seeing another man, if I wasn't ready to date. I need to run away from Bull and yet, here I am glad to see him. You would think my past would have zapped all the stupidity out of me.

Apparently not.

Chapter 12

BULL

"HAVEN'T YOU CAUSED enough trouble for one day?" Skye asks me.

She looks so tired...she looks *sad*. I don't want that. I like Doc with fire in her eyes. Hell, I don't even mind when she's spitting it at me. It turns me on. Then again, everything she does seems to do that.

"I saw you running up the stairs, I wanted to check on you."

"Not right now, Bull. It's late, and I've had a bad day," she says, turning away from me.

I can't resist. I know I've pushed her hard, but I can't stop. Fuck, I tried to stay away, but I needed her. That kiss we just shared, the time we've spent together? It's all just made my initial attraction to her stronger. *I need this woman.* I come up behind her, placing my hands on her shoulders, and rub the spot in her neck that is tight with tension.

"I know I have a lot to overcome with you, Doc. I get that. The way we met was fucked up. But I think I'm doing a damn good job of proving myself to you."

"Bull..."

"Skye, you can't tell me there isn't a pull between us. Something that draws us towards each other."

"It's just hormones," she says, her head dropping down with a sigh of relief, as I continue my massage.

My hand trembles, but I ignore the weakness, and concentrate instead on touching the woman I've been dreaming about.

"Bullshit. There's a fire between us, Skye. It's not something you will find with someone else. *Especially that fucker Walter.*"

She tenses up again at the mention of Walter, and I instantly regret saying his name.

"Bull…"

"Skye, give me a chance. Give *us* a chance."

"Bull, you are a risk, I have Matty to think about. I've made so many mistakes before…"

"Doc, you've read my file. You know about the fire and the attack."

"Yeah," her voice whispers, "I know."

"I have these headaches. So bad sometimes, they can practically rob my vision. I've heard of blinding headaches, but I didn't know shit about them."

"Did you see a neurologist?"

"Yeah, Doc. I'm okay, just fucked in the head apparently."

"Bull," she says and tries to turn around, but I don't let her.

"Listen, Doc. I want to tell you this shit, I do. I can promise you the man you have in your head the drugged out thug who doesn't take care of his dick, that's not the man I am. The man I can show you, if you just give me a chance. I got my HIV/AIDS test back and I'm clean. I have the report and I'm even willing to keep getting tested until you feel comfortable. I don't have a problem with that, but it's time we move forward here."

"We don't really know each other, and we sure don't fit into each other's worlds. I don't think I'm the kind of woman you want. I've had two lovers in my lifetime. Heck, that's a slow day for you."

I pull her around, holding her face to bring her eyes to mine.

"I never want to hear about the men who came before me, Skye. They don't exist."

"What? Are you…"

"I may not be your first, but I *will be* your fucking last. Do you think I would jump through these hoops for anyone?"

"I…You don't know me!"

"No, not as good as I want. But I will, and I can promise you something else, Doc."

"You can?" she asks, and fuck it's all I can do not to kiss her.

"I'm with you. My dick will not be anywhere else, Doc. You don't have to worry about that."

"You're so romantic," she grumbles, but I can see a little of the woman who goes head-to-head with me returning. I like her better than the sad woman that was here when I first came to the roof.

"Give this a chance, Skye. Trust me."

"I want to…"

She wraps her arms around her body, shivering. I take off my cut and put it on her shoulders, without thinking. Just like so much, it's a gut instinct with this woman.

"What are you doing?" she asks, but she doesn't fight me when I settle the heavy leather on her arms. In fact, she takes the two ends in one hand and holds it together at her chest.

"You're cold," I answer and my tone is gruff. She looks fucking good in Savage MC leather. She looks like she was made for it. *Made for me.*

"You're a little crazy."

"I bet I can make you like crazy," I tell her before I move my hand to caress her neck, loving the way her skin feels against my fingers. Then, I bring her lips to mine and claim them.

Chapter 13

SKYE

"**M**OM! YOU'RE HOME!" Matty says when I climb into his bed. His arms go around me and I breathe in his scent. He's getting so big. He's nine now. It's been a struggle having him in my life, but without him I wouldn't have survived. He keeps me going. Matty is my reason for getting up in the morning.

"You should be asleep, pumpkin. You got school tomorrow," I tell him, when I settle him back against the pillows.

His warm little body curls into mine. My fingers trace over the sleeve of his Teenage Mutant Ninja Turtles pajamas. I wish I could freeze this moment and so many others like it. With my residency in full swing now, I get such little quality time with Matty. I hate it. I hate every minute of it. I look down at his sweet face, and his head full of dark hair. He looks almost nothing like me, he even somehow managed to escape my red hair. He has one mark on him that warms me though when I see it. He and I have the same exact birthmark. It looks like a small star on the back of our right ear. It's ours and ours alone.

I feel guilty that he's been having trouble at school. It's hard being the new kid at any age, but by the age of nine friendships have been formed, and it's hard to break into the different cliques. I still think this move was the best thing for him—for us. It doesn't stop the guilt, though. He doesn't have a father, so he's already different from other kids. There hasn't been a male figure to teach him sports, to bond with. All of that's my fault and it makes me worry about letting Bull into our lives. Is he going to be another bad mistake, and one that hurts my son? He's already dealing with bullies. I've held him and dried his tears, but each tear makes me feel like I've done more to hurt the child I care about more than anything in the world.

"I don't go to school tomorrow," Matty thankfully interrupts my thoughts.

"You don't?"

"No, remember? Tomorrow is the intermural soccer games at school. You said I could miss it and you'd take me to the zoo! Did you forget, Mom? Do you have to work?" he questions, too young to keep the accusation out of his voice—hurting me with it. How many times have I let him down? The frequency has definitely increased with med school, and now residency.

I hug him close and look up at the ceiling in his room, feeling ashamed. I had forgotten. Even worse, in the back of my mind I'm dreading it, because I'm just so exhausted. I had plans for lying around in my pajamas and doing nothing.

"I didn't forget," I lie. "I was just testing you to see if you remembered. I've been thinking about seeing the monkeys all day."

"Monkeys? Mom that's so lame. Charles said they have turtles that are bigger than elephants!"

"Charles might be stretching things a little."

"No. He's been to the zoo like a million times."

"Well then, I can't wait," I smile. "As long as just the turtles are big, and not the snakes."

"I want a pet snake."

"I know and remember what I told you about that?"

"Yeah, but I keep hoping you'll change your mind."

"I don't think that will ever happen, buddy."

He laughs and wraps his arm around my stomach. I lie there listening to him breathe. It's the best sound in the entire world.

"You want a story?" I ask, already knowing the answer.

"Yeah the one about King Matthew."

I smile and tell him our shortened rendition of the sword in the stone. I've told it so many times, I don't even have to think while doing it. The words roll from my tongue like I'm on autopilot and, as always, about half way through Matty goes out for the night. I lie there a little longer, enjoying the moment. I'm almost asleep when I hear a knock on the door. It's almost ten thirty, and I never get much company. I figure Blair might have forgot something, when she left earlier. I ease off the bed, place a small kiss on my baby's forehead, arrange the covers over him, before going to the door.

When I look out the peephole, my body goes tight. I leave the chain locked and open the door slightly. I find myself staring at the very last person I wanted to see tonight.

Chapter 14

SKYE

"WALTER, WHAT ARE you doing here?" I ask, even though I know in my gut why he is here and I'm not happy.

"We needed to talk, Skye."

I look at him, I mean *really* look at him. He's not bad looking. He actually pretty good looking. He's forty-two and with just a hint of gray in his hair. He's clean-shaven and looks impeccably put together in his suit and tie. He's everything I should probably want and look for in a man, but he leaves me cold. That's the real reason I've never returned any of his offers to date. That's the reason I've tried to keep my distance personally from him. I will admit I had weakened in that stance a few months back. I toyed with the idea of making a stable home for Matty. Walter was the lead candidate, because of his profession, and his understanding of the hours of dedication it takes to be a good doctor. There would be less adjustment with Walter. On paper it all made sense. I was so close to accepting a date with him.

Then a man walked into my exam room and reminded me of the feelings a woman has when she is attracted to a man. He was all wrong for me, and I should never go there with him—logically. But Bull's right. There's a fire between us, a raging inferno of attraction that I've never felt before with anyone else. Realistically, I miss sex. I miss it bad, and even with the long drought I've had, the thought of sex with Walter leaves me feeling…cold and maybe a little nauseated. Looking at him now, that feeling only intensifies. He might be right for me on paper, but he's nowhere close to it in person.

"It's late Walter, and I've not had a break in over two days, I really…"

"It will just take a minute."

I sigh. It's apparent he's not going to leave quietly. I close the door, unlatch the chain, before opening it back up to let him in. I close the door, leaning against it to shore up what little energy I have left. I'm so tired. I want nothing more than to crawl into my bed, and sleep. Finally, I move away, leading Walter to the sofa. I sit first and he follows.

"What's between you and that man? Mr. Kane?" he asks, getting straight to the point.

"I don't think that's something you really have a right asking, Walter."

"You know I have feelings for you Skye. We've been getting closer these last few months, working so near each other. There are feelings between us."

His hand trails down the side of my face and it sends chills through me—but not the good kind. *These are cold.* I resist the urge to turn away from him, but I do pull back.

"I wasn't aware you felt like that Walter," I lie. "You never said so directly. I assumed your invitations were merely offers between professional colleagues, with likeminded interests."

I'm a little amazed at how easy the lies roll from my tongue. It's easier to pretend though that the times he has asked me out, I have misunderstood. I'm hoping he might let it go with that and let me out of this horrible conversation.

"You were mistaken then, Skye. You're a beautiful woman. We have much in common, I admire your heart, and how much you have achieved in your life. I want to get to know you better, on a more personal level."

So much for getting out of the conversation.

"Walter, I wish I had known, but now…"

"You can't be seeing that hoodlum, Skye. Surely you can see you are far above his reach," Walter says, interrupting me.

I think that was supposed to be a compliment from him, but it doesn't feel like one. *It sits wrong.* It upsets me. *It pisses me off.* I might not think Bull is a good risk, but hearing Walter talk as if we are better than Bull, makes me want to lash out. The insinuation is there in Walter's words, and it's extremely clear he feels he is far and above Bull.

"That's not true, Walter. In fact, Bull has been very good to me."

"Please, Skye. I understand hormones, but for you to lower yourself to that man's level, is preposterous."

His statement leaves me speechless. I'd love to say what I really think, but I'm trying really hard to remember that this is my boss.

"Walter, I'm upset that you would insinuate such a thing. Further…"

"Surely you see that it is what it seems like, Skye. To allow that filthy…"

"I think you should stop there. I happen to like Mr. Kane."

"You can't feel anything for him, you're too different. And what about your son? How can you find this thug a respectable role model for him?"

He hits on the one thing that worries me the most, but right now, all I can think is what an asshole Walter is. I want him out of my house.

"I think you've said enough tonight. I need some rest," I tell him—intent on nothing more than getting him to leave.

He stands, but he doesn't go to the door like I expected. Instead, he pulls me into him, with a strong hand on my neck. Then, before I can stop him, he kisses me. The first thought I have is that his kiss is nothing like Bull's. No, Walter's kiss leaves me cold. His taste is slightly acidic. I can even taste the hint of onions. My insides recoil. This is proof-positive that there is no way I should ever encourage his attentions. On paper he might be the better choice for stability with Matty, but in reality, he is all kinds of wrong for me. Something tells me the same would be true for my son.

His tongue pushes into my mouth and I want to gag. I push against his shoulders, trying to break free. His hand is at my chest, and I feel it dive inside my shirt to cup my breast. I push harder, finally getting my mouth away from him. He starts biting on my shoulder, and I suck in air to keep from vomiting.

"Walter stop! I don't want this!" I growl, apparently the full moon tonight has caused him to lose his ever-loving-mind.

"Give us a chance, Skye. We could be good together. This could be so good." He says, but even his voice sounds cold to me. His head goes down, and before he can lay his lips anywhere else, I push him hard.

"I said...No!" I growl, he goes back a couple of steps when I shove him. My shirt tears—just slightly, but I feel cold air hit my body. I pay no mind to it though, just relieved because Walter's hand is no longer on my breast.

"What the fuck is going on here?"

My head jerks up, and I look at the front door. Suddenly, I get the name behind the man, because in this moment, he is a bull seeing red and ready to charge.

Crap.

Chapter 15

BULL

I HEAR SKYE'S cry from outside.

I was debating whether to come in or not. I pushed Skye pretty hard today. Fuck, my head is kind of screwed up lately. It has been, since the mess with Carrie. Something about Skye throws me off kilter and I just got tired of waiting. Now, I'm starting to have second thoughts about pushing her.

Why should Skye give me a shot? She sure as hell deserves better than me. I've been a fucked up mess for so long now, I'm not sure I remember who I was before. Dragon feels guilty over the attack at Dancer's. He shouldn't. That's on me, it's all mine. I was drunk. If I hadn't been, the fucker would have never gotten the drop on me. I never told my brothers that, and I got Melissa to help bury the toxicology results the hospital ran. That's my dirty little secret. Fuck, it seems like I've been searching for something to get lost in forever now. The bottom of a bottle, pills…women. *I disgust myself.*

And what if I'm wrong? What if I backslide? I've been clean for six months, sure—but it's been a fucking hard ride. That's the main reason I haven't pressed Doc, but today I snapped. I couldn't stand the waiting anymore, and I went caveman on her. She probably thinks I'm a desperate fucker who has to chase women down. God, is that who I am now? I should just tell her goodbye, find my motherfucking balls, and walk away. I shouldn't have to force her to spend time with me. That's really why I'm here, and I had every intention of telling her that—*until I hear her scream.*

I open her door to find *Walter-boy* and Skye standing way too close together. Skye looks extremely pissed and more than a little scared.

"What the fuck is going on here?" I'm trying to stay calm, but I notice the top of Skye's shirt is torn. *I go off.*

I grab Walter by his scrawny throat, and wrap my hand around it. I'm going to end this motherfucker. What would have happened if I hadn't been here? I'm going to choke the life out of this miserable fucker. Nah, that's too easy. I'll cut off his dick, force-feed it to him and *then* choke the life out of him.

I slam him up against the wall and hear something fall. Then there is the sound of glass breaking. Out of the corner of my eye, I see a picture lying on the floor beside me.

"Who the fuck said you could put your hands on my woman?" I yell at the asshole, ready to tear him apart. Skye hits my bad arm with a....Fuck! She hit me with a bible! And not just any bible, it's a hardback and looks like it belongs on an altar at church or something.

"Fucking hell, Doc!"

"Let go of him! What are you doing?"

"Teaching Walter-boy some manners so he'll know to never put his hands on you? *You're welcome by the way.*"

"I had it under control! What in the hell are you doing here?"

"I wanted to see you."

Her head snaps back like I slapped her. Then she looks back at Walter-boy.

She touches my arm and quietly says, "Let him go, Bull."

Now normally I would have ignored her, but she did something good here. She touched me. That makes me feel charitable, so I drop him.

"What are you doing?" she cries, bending down to help the asshole to his feet. He pushes her away and stands up.

"You said to let him go. Maybe you should ask him what he was doing?"

"I was kissing her, you moron," he says, adjusting his suit.

Yeah, there went my generosity. I introduce his lying mouth to my fist. He falls back down with a thud.

"Kissing doesn't involve a woman screaming no, asshole," I tell him, and I'm congratulating myself on being so calm.

"Bull! I'm so sorry, Walter. Perhaps it would be best if you leave. We can talk about this tomorrow when…"

"What the fuck are you apologizing to him for? You weren't trying to force yourself on his sorry ass. There will be no talking about it tomorrow. You're going to stay away from Skye, and treat her with the utmost respect from now on, right, *Walter*?"

"Real classy guy you've aligned yourself with Dr. Walker," Walter says.

"You remember that before you try anything else, or even try to talk to her, asshole. I can bury your body in places no one will think to look. You get me, right?"

"Bull! Walter, he's not serious. We'll discuss this…"

"I'm deadly serious. *Try me, Walter. Try me, one time*," I tell him, crossing my arms.

He looks at Skye, then back at me, then leaves, slamming the door hard.

"I can't believe you!" She huffs at me, and goddamn she looks beautiful, even if she wants to kill me right now.

"I can't either," I tell her.

"You just can't come in here…wait… what?"

"I can't believe I let that asshole walk out of here. You got me going soft, Doc." I let my hand go down and adjust my dick. I grin as she watches the movement, and when her eyes come back to mine, I wink. "Well not all of me."

Chapter 16

SKYE

"YOU ARE COMPLETELY insane!" I bark at him. He is, the only problem is I *like* what he just did. I can't remember anyone ever standing up for me. Here is this man doing it without even being asked. I'm not sure how to react and on top of that there's Walter. I may like what Bull did, *privately*. Walter might have been so far out of line that there was no way to recover, but he *is* my boss. My *very* vindictive boss and Bull just threatened to kill him. No, correction he threatened to bury him where no one would ever think to look. What do I do with this? What do I do with Bull?

"Mom?"

I turn to see Matty coming down the hall, rubbing the sleep out of his eyes. The familiar tug at my heart hits me. Just seeing my baby infuses me with pride. We may not have had an easy time of it, but I don't regret a minute of it.

"I'm sorry sweetie, did we wake you?" I ask him, getting down on my knees, so I can hold him close and ruffle his hair.

"I heard yelling," he says looking at Bull. "Who are you?"

"He's…"

"I'm a friend of your Mama's. You, Matthew?"

I watch as my son straightens his back and looks Bull over like he's seeking out everything he can find out about him.

"Yeah. Were you yelling at my Mom?"

Bull smiles widely, almost proudly, at Matty. He's given me cocky grins and flirty looks before, but I don't think I've ever seen a genuine smile from him before, until right now. The fact that he gave it to Matty means more than I could say. Maybe that was the exact moment I decided to soften. Up until this point, I was just fighting an unexplainable attraction for a man I should in no way be attracted to. Now? *Now*, I think there might be more to this attraction than just hormones.

"Horse feathers…," I mumble.

"What's that Doc?"

"Mom always says horse feathers when she gets upset."

Bull laughs, "Or Christ's toenails?"

"Sometimes," Matty says and I feel myself blush. "Did you yell at my mom?"

"No, there was someone else here, but I got rid of him."

"You like my mom?" Matty asks, and I hold my head down. I want to interject, but I don't know what to say. What can I say? *Sorry Matty, this can't be the daddy you've been asking me for, because he's a player who is just now recovering from a disease you get when you bump uglies with another person without protection.* I don't think that would work.

"More every minute."

Damn it, why does he have to be so sweet *and* be an ass?

"Let's get you back in bed, baby. We leave for the zoo awful early. You need your rest."

"You want to go to the zoo with us?" Matty asks, and I wish the ground would swallow me up.

"Mr. Kane, can't…"

"I'd love to. I love the zoo. I'm a big turtle fan."

"Me too!"

I shoot Bull a look that could freeze Lake Michigan harder

than any winter storm. He just gives me another cocky grin. I'm starting to hate those. I know he looked at Matty's pajamas. *Jerk-face*. He ignores my look.

"Let's get you to bed," I say again, leading him back to his room.

"I'll see you in the morning, Matthew."

"Later…Hey! What's your name?"

"Bull."

"Bull like the animal?" Matty asks.

"That's it."

"Cool! See you tomorrow Bull."

"Bye, little dude."

I say nothing. All I can think of, over and over are words I can't say around Matty. Sometimes *horse feathers* just isn't a strong enough expletive.

Damn.

Chapter 17

BULL

I T'S THE FIRST of November and it should be cold, or at the very least, cool. Not today. Today, Mother Nature decided to be a bitch and bless the state of Tennessee with a heatwave. Since we drove down to Knoxville to spend the day at the zoo, you would think that would make this the most miserable day I've had in my life. It's not. I can't remember having a better day in my life. Skye and her son…

Hell, I was intrigued by her before, but after today I'm pretty much gone for the woman. I used to think Dragon and Crusher were pussies for falling for their women so hard, but hell if Skye gives me the opening, she's never getting rid of me.

I was afraid the reason I was attracted to Skye in the beginning was because she reminded me of Carrie. The more I get to know her, I realize she's nothing like Carrie. The color of their hair—that's it. Skye has more grit. Where I felt the need to be gentle all the time with Carrie, Skye is like electricity to my system. She can be mouthy as all hell, and it makes me itch to grab her, push her against the wall, and fuck her into submission. Then I watch her with her boy, and see the way she takes care of him. Fuck, even that makes my dick grow hard. I want a taste of her, I want her fussing over me. Hell, I even wonder how she'd be with a kid we had together. This leads me to imagining her pregnant with my baby and I get a fucking hard-on just thinking about her stomach tight with my baby, her tits swollen. All of this means I've pretty much spent the day walking around with a cock hard enough to bust through concrete.

"You're looking tired sweetheart," Skye's voice grabs my attention. So motherfucking sweet my teeth hurt. I've got to have a taste of her.

"Mom, I'm okay. I just want to see the kangaroos!"

I watch Skye, and I know she's been working a ton of overtime. She's worn out. It amazes me that with all of her responsibilities, she still manages to be such a great mom.

"Hey Matthew, I'm dying of thirst man. How about we stop in the food court and grab a bite to eat and then head to the Down Under exhibit? I'm an old man, you have to have a little mercy on me," I joke, determined to get Skye a small rest.

Matty's shrewd eyes are looking at me and he knows what I'm about. I can see it. So I cave and point towards his mom, giving him a wink. He looks over and sighs, but then nods back, smiling.

"Okay, Bull. I could use a cherry slushy anyways."

"Cherry? Man that's whack. Lime is where it's at."

"You're both wrong, it's raspberry," Skye chimes in.

"Raspberry?" Matthew and I both ask her—like she's crazy.

"That's just gross, Mom."

"It's not even a real color," I add.

"It's a fruit!" she defends.

"Not a very good one," I come back with a smile, as the three of us walk over to the tables. I leave them there, waving off Skye's attempt at giving me money. Damn woman has a huge independent streak. It's cute, but she has no idea who she's dealing with. *It's going to be fun, showing her.*

"What is that?" she asks when I come back to the table.

"One of life's greatest pleasures," I tell her, winking at Matthew while handing him a chili-dog.

"Oh man! Thanks, Bull!"

I hand one over to Skye, and then sit down beside her.

"This doesn't look healthy," she says, but she's licking her lips. She's been doing it all for so long by herself, I think she's forgotten how to enjoy herself. I still feel like I should have let her go, but that's off the table now. I'm just going to bust my ass trying to be a better man.

"C'mon, Doc. Live a little."

"Yeah, Mom! Live a little!" Matty joins in.

That's probably when it happens. Skye laughs—not just a little, but a lot. She laughs hard. I'm frozen with the damn hot dog half way to my mouth, and all I can do is watch her and hear the joy coming from her. It's beautiful. Then I look over to Matty, and see the chili running down his face, as he's stuffing the damn thing in his mouth. He forgets to take the time to breathe, and I can't help but laugh too. That's probably when I fall completely for her. *Maybe.*

"Slow down there, sport. Take time to enjoy it. I'll get you another one if you're still hungry."

"Really?" he asks like it's Christmas morning. "What about mom?"

I look over at Skye and she looks at the two of us and then takes a huge bite of her hot dog too, licking some of the chili off her lip when she's done. *My poor dick.*

"I want another one too," she says with a grin. Matty giggles and goes back to eating.

He must forget about wanting seconds, because one of the traveling workers comes to the line just beyond the tables, with a green wing macaw. Kids are gathering around to watch the bird and to feed it peanuts.

"Can I go over there, Mom? Please?"

"Don't go any further," Skye tells him. He nods his head yes, while running to the kids already there. It's then she lets the worry come back into her face.

"He's fine, Doc."

"I know. I just worry."

"You need to unwind. Matthew's good, Doc. He's a happy kid."

"I worry over everything. I've made so many mistakes, I try to make sure I don't misstep now. I forget I need to let Matty have a life sometimes too. I'm sorry. You were right. I need to live a little."

"I get it. You're a Mama, and from what I can see a damned good one.

"Bull, about last night…well all of it really…"

I put my hand along the side of her neck and pull her to me, so I can look in her eyes.

"I want your body, Doc. I want it so fucking bad, I'm having fucking wet dreams about it. But regardless of what you think, I don't have to buy a woman's interest. What I'm feeling for you woman, is special. Today has been one of the best days I can ever remember having."

"It has been for me too, Bull."

"That has to mean something, right?"

"Can, we take it day-by-day?"

"That sounds good to me."

"You're wrong you know," she says, licking her lips and I swear it's all I can do not to attack her right there. How much is a man supposed to stand?

"What do you mean?" I ask, mentally apologizing to my

balls.

"I'm starting to have a very good impression of you," she whispers, leaning further into me.

Her tongue darts out and caresses against my bottom one. I suck it in briefly, then let it go.

"Are you trying to seduce me, Doc?"

"I think I might be," she answers, and I let my thumb pet the pounding pulse point along the side of her neck.

"I'm not sure that's a smart thing to do," I warn her, because if she lets me in, I'm not letting her go.

"C'mon, Bull. Live dangerously," she taunts and that seals her fate. The last thought I have before I take over the kiss, is this is when it *really* happens.

I'm not falling. I've fell completely. I'm gone over this woman.

AW

I GOT OFF work to watch Skye today. I knew she would want me close. It was there in the look she gave me yesterday when we talked. She hides so much from the world, but I see it. I see it in her eyes. She needs me. I wasn't prepared for *him*. He's been panting after her for way too long. She won't let him touch her. She's too pure for someone like him.

I know it. It's the one thing that drew me to her from the beginning. I just needed to make sure the time was right to make my move. You can't rush connections like ours.

I go cold, as she bends over to hug her child. I don't like that she has him. I almost decided to walk away when I found out. The more I was around her though, I came to realize that even she could make mistakes. I certainly did with my last choice. Skye is different. She will be forever. I will have to disperse of the child. That's regrettable. He might be a good kid, but he can't come between our love, Skye and I need time together. No one else around. Just the two of us learning the path to pleasure. I will need all of her attention for her training.

Mr. Kane will have to go and soon. He is distracting her. I know who he is. It wouldn't be wise to alert his friends to me. But if he doesn't back away, I may have to speed my plans up. I may have to take Skye away from all of the distractions and begin her training early.

My heartbeat thunders in my ears, and anger funnels through me, when he kisses her. That shouldn't have happened. Skye should have known better. Now she will have to be punished before her training begins. I will have to break her. I didn't want it to be this way. *She left me with no choice.*

Chapter 18

SKYE

I PULL THE door until it's just cracked after getting Matty settled, then walk back into the living room. Bull is sitting on my couch and he's so big, he makes my streamlined couch look small. He also looks really good on it. Dang.

"Did you get him settled?"

"Yeah, he was completely worn out," I tell him, standing in the middle of the room, unsure of what to do. It's been such a good day, and I've really let my guard down with Bull, but now, *I'm nervous.*

"Come sit down, Doc," Bull says, patting the couch beside him.

I take a breath and sit down. I worry about what to do when I get there. Do I sit on the edge and give us plenty of room, do I sit next to him? In the end, I didn't need to worry. The minute I sit down Bull takes over. He pulls me so I'm lying against his side and we're curled up. He has the television on and the volume turned down low, to an old black and white movie.

"You like old movies?" I ask him, watching the screen, but enjoying the way the heat from his body seeps into me.

"They're okay. You don't?"

"Honestly? Unless it's Matty's cartoons the television never comes on."

"No television?"

"Nah. I like reading, or napping. Napping is always good."

He flips the TV off and pulls me so I'm lying completely over top of him. His hand plays with my hair, relaxing me.

"I tell you what, Doc. You can nap on me anytime," he says softly. I think if I let myself, I could drown in the dark pools of his eyes.

"Generous of you."

"I thought so," he laughs.

"I had a good time today, Bull."

"I did too, Doc."

"You're different than I thought you would be."

"Well given my track record you can't have a good impression of me."

"Umm…"

He smiles and gives me a squeeze.

"It's okay, Doc. I didn't exactly leave a good impression with you. I would like to explain, if you want."

"The pills?"

"That's what worries you the most?"

"Yeah. I mean, I know addiction is something you can overcome, but you can also go back to it, and I have Matty…I don't want you to get mad at me Bull. But…" she starts, and then has to take a breath—I should have prepared myself, "I'd be lying if I said I'm comfortable about it."

I'm afraid I'm hurting him and I don't want to. But somewhere over the last few times I've spent with Bull, I've decided to take a chance…or at least try. If I do, then there are things I need to be open and honest with him about.

"We've talked about the attack and the headaches. I was having trouble dealing with the pain and tremors, I had just lost a woman I...cared about and I let her down...let my brothers down. Then, I lost someone I was in the service with. He wanted me to help him and I couldn't, I chose my club because they needed me too. Hell, Doc the list just goes on...it was stupid. It all sounds like an excuse for someone who was weak. I don't even know how or why it started. *It just did.* I can only promise you, I'm not that man now."

"I'm sorry you went through all of that, Bull," I whisper, letting my fingers brush along the side of his face. I can't stop myself from placing a kiss on his chest, above his heart. He gives me another squeeze. Does he know that when he gets this look in his eyes it makes me want to hold him close, and make the sadness go away? "What was her name?"

"Carrie," he says and it's wrong—all kinds of wrong, but I find myself jealous over the woman who he lost. How old was she? She must have died young. I have a hundred questions about her, but they're all selfish, and I don't want him to talk about her. I selfishly don't even want him missing her, so I concentrate on the other things he said.

"You said you chose your club? I don't guess I really understand that much about your club, other than you seem close to them. Growing up my Dad was part of the Shriners, is it kind of like that? A place where men meet, let off steam, and do work for charity?"

His face gets the strangest look on it. He looks as if he is in shock. His body tenses up under me.

"Shit," he mutters.

"Bull?"

"Skye you said you like to read. Haven't you ever read anything about motorcycle clubs in your reading or something? *Anything?*"

"As a student and even now in my residency, textbooks

and charts are about all I have time to read, why?"

Again that look comes across his face. I'm starting to worry. What exactly is this club? I mean, I've heard of big motorcycle gangs, criminals really, but it's been glamourized for television, I'm sure. He can't be part of that kind of group. Fear grips my heart. I have Matty to think of. Hell, I have myself to think about here. He can't be part of a gang.

Can he?

Chapter 19

BULL

FUCK! I DIDN'T see this becoming a problem. I just assumed she knew about the Savage Brothers. I figured she knew what it meant. I already have two strikes against me with this woman. Will this be the fucking third? I'm scrambling, racking my brain, trying to figure out how to approach this.

"I live in a different world than you, Skye," I start vague, because I'm not diving into what we do exactly. *I can't.* Hell, no member tells his old lady the specifics in the first place, and in the second, as much as it kills me, I can't trust Skye with information about the brothers right now.

"I'm starting to see that," she says, and I nearly groan at this latest road block I have with Skye.

"I know you don't have experience with the club world, but still you *must* have heard *something* about the Savage Brothers since moving here. Or hell, at least heard about motorcycle clubs enough to know the basics."

"Not really. It's never been a life I've had a lot of interest in. Though, something Melissa mentioned does stick in my mind. She said that I didn't know how to satisfy you, that as club members her and the other girls…"

"That bitch is not a member of the club, Skye. She's definitely not one of the girls the club keeps."

"Keeps?" she asks, and I'm not sure what to make of her tone.

Again, I don't really want to get into any of it. I could kill Melissa. Hell, Dragon might. Right now I need to worry about Skye. I don't need to give her any other reasons to say no to me. I decide to tackle the thing that worries her the most right now.

"You're worried about how many women I've had sex with, but it's not exactly that many. It's just..."

"You're a man-whore?" she adds helpfully.

"The club keeps women, we take care of them—they take care of us. Mutual benefits I guess."

She tenses up and fuck me, I wish I could take the words back.

"Take care? You mean you keep women just for sex? Like those BDSM clubs?"

I shake my head. Jesus. This shouldn't be so hard. Did Dragon or Crusher have these problems? Hell, I don't think Dance has clued Carrie into everything. *Maybe I should have followed his lead?*

"No, I mean they like our lifestyle. They work at the club, they entertain the men, keep us happy. Don't get that look, Doc. The women want this life. They enjoy it. We live a hard life and hell, Skye... *It's just the way it is.*"

Why does that sound so lame to my ears? I'm making a fucking mess of this.

"So you keep prostitutes?"

"They're not prostitutes, Skye."

"They give you sex in exchange for a home, food and money?"

"If you want to think of it like that, I guess you could. But that's not what it's about."

"Whatever. So, you have club prostitutes and you go around and have unprotected sex with them anytime you want. Got it," she says, and starts to pull away.

I hold onto her with a sigh. I can't let her go.

"It's not the way you're making it sound, not really. And there are members of the club that have old ladies. Dragon is married now."

"Old ladies?"

"Girlfriends—wives."

"And how do these women feel about the club prostitutes?"

"They're called Twinkies."

"Excuse me?"

"Twinkies, that's what we call them."

"*Delightful.* So you name your prostitutes after snack cakes."

"Skye." *Fuck. I'm an idiot. Why did I decide to talk about this again?*

"I think I'm about talked out, Bull. Maybe we could pick this up some other night," she says, and I let her go this time, because maybe she's right.

"Okay, Doc. When? I could come over tomorrow and…"

"How about half past never?" she says, getting up and walking towards the door.

I rub the back of my neck, because I've had pain there all day, but the thought of leaving here and letting Skye get away, not only increases my tension, it ramps up the headache. Listening to her describe my lifestyle causes a war inside of me. On one hand, I'm pissed off that she can't appreciate the family I have, and on the other, I'm ashamed of the way she makes it sound. It's not that way…*not really*…I just don't know how to make her understand.

"Doc, I'm not explaining this really well. How about I take you to the club tomorrow evening when you get off work? You can meet Dragon, Nicole and some of the other members. If, after you see how they are with each other, you don't like my lifestyle? I'll walk away. I won't push you."

It hurts to say that, but it's true. I want Skye, but I can't give up my family. I need her to see what I do when I look at the club. Good people. Caring people. *A family*.

She stops and sighs, then asks me a question that I had somehow forgot we were discussing.

"Even if I do like your lifestyle, and let me warn you Bull, that's like a huge '*what if*.' But even if I do, that still doesn't help us figure out where we go from here. You're a recovering…"

I don't want to hear her call me an addict. I can't. I can't hear those words from her lips. So I kiss her before the words can escape. Before she can deny me further, I take two large steps, and I'm there. Then, my lips are on hers, my tongue is in her mouth, her taste is inside me, my arms are full of her, and her hands are holding me. That's all I want to concentrate on. My hands latch onto her sweet round ass, kneading it, and pulling her into me. She's stiff, but still I take over her mouth, my tongue savors her, and I am lost in her. She softens, her hands go around me, and her nails bite into my back.

It's a good kiss. *A fucking good kiss*. And when she moves restlessly against me, I break away to let my lungs take in air. Her face is flushed, and her lips are swollen. I didn't shave this morning, and the stubble from my face has scratched her and I like it. *A hell of a lot*.

"If you like my club woman, all bets are off."

"Bull, everything I know about addiction says you shouldn't even think of starting a relationship for at least a year. Especially while you are in recovery."

"I'm not waiting a fucking year to have you, Doc."

"Bull…"

I grab her hair, wrapping my fist in it, tightening my hold, so she can see how serious I am.

"I am not waiting a fucking year to have you, Skye. Woman, today was one of the best days of my life."

"Mine too," she says, simply.

"Then you have to know that I am not giving you up. I can do this Skye. Trust me. C'mon Doc, sometimes you have to live a little." She studies me, but doesn't respond. "Take a chance on me, Doc. I won't let you regret it."

I have never felt such relief in my life as I do when she nods yes. Then, I slam my lips back onto hers and kiss her until we both forget our names.

I pray I can just get her to see my club like I see it. Hell, I can't remember praying, but I pray all of the way home. I need for Skye to give us a chance. I can't imagine living my life without her or my brothers. I just hope like hell it doesn't come to that.

AW

SHE HAD HER chance. I watch as that man's taillights disappear. He's really starting to be annoying. I watched them through the window, I was sure Skye was going to do the right thing. She didn't. I can't keep waiting. I'm not ready to bring her home yet. There are still things to accomplish to make it perfect. I am going to have to step up my game though. I need to get my message across to Skye.

It is decided.

I will send her one more message, and then if she still refuses to fall into line, I will have to bring her to heel. I tighten my grip on the black silk panties I got from her house earlier. I bring them to my nose. Bile rolls in my stomach. It is not her pure scent now—it's changed. *She has changed.*

I must work faster, before she ruins it all.

Before she ruins things, just like the others did.

I have to hurry.

Chapter 20

BULL

"DOC? YOU OKAY?" We're sitting in the car outside of the club, and she's barely said three words since we left. She's definitely nervous, but I'm worried it's something else.

"What if they hate me?"

"They won't."

"What if I hate them?"

I don't really know how to answer that, since at this point it's the biggest worry I have.

"Just give them a chance, Doc. That's all I ask."

She nods, and I get out of the car. She has the door opened by the time I get to her side, but I manage to be there in time to help her out. I hate driving a car. I want Skye on my bike. But until we see how today goes, I'm not going to put her on the back of it. I have a feeling that if this goes south, she'll haunt everything around me. The last thing I need is to climb on the back of my girl, and remember Skye there.

I keep my hand on Skye's back as I lead her to the club entrance. I try to imagine what the place looks like to someone who is just seeing it for the first time, but that's impossible for me. The club is wrapped up in everything I am, and has been home for so long, just the sight of it calms me. I look down at Skye, to try and gage her reaction, but other than the way those perfect white teeth are gnawing into the corner of her bottom lip, there's not a clue as to what she is thinking. Hopefully her nerves will calm. We pass by one of the new recruits guarding the door, I think I've heard the boys call him Circus. I really don't want to know what shit earned him that road name.

He opens the door for us and Skye thanks him. He gives her a once over and I *accidentally* elbow him as I pass—in the throat. He's not getting my vote when the time comes, motherfucking little bitch. Skye is so wrapped up in her nerves that she doesn't even notice the exchange.

The club is quiet today, and to be honest that might be why I picked it to begin with. I sure as hell wasn't bringing her here during a party. Dragon and Nicole are in the back talking to Dancer. Carrie isn't here, and I'm glad. Doc doesn't need anything else to think about right now. I lead her over to the table, they look up and holy hell, this whole thing feels awkward as fuck.

"Hey Bull. Is this the Doctor we've been hearing about?" Nicole, bless her heart speaks up first to break the silence.

"Yeah, little Mama. Skye this is Nicole. For some reason she decided to marry Dragon there, and that other ugly fucker is Dancer."

"Hi," Skye responds. She has her hands clasped at her waist and the grip she has on them is turning her skin completely white. *Shit!* This is not going well.

"You got a problem with Bull being a member of the club?" Dragon asks and I'd like to strangle him.

"Dragon, lay the fuck off."

"What? I've got a right to ask the question. You've been worrying like a motherfucker hoping this chick fits in. Hell, it's all you talked about last night. It's my club, so I want to know what in the hell the problem is."

"Would it matter if I did?"

"It would to him."

"Then I guess that's between Bull and me to work out."

"Do you know who I am?"

"Other than your name is apparently Dragon, no, I don't."

"Let me ask you something, why do you think you're good enough for my boy?"

"Dragon, man…" I try again to stop him. I can understand why he's questioning Skye, but I don't need more strikes against me.

"It's okay, Bull. Let him have his say."

"Yeah Bull, let me have my say," Dragon chimes mockingly, and I flip him off.

"Are you an ass to everyone? Or am I just lucky, Dragon?" Skye asks, and everyone stops moving.

"Skye, you can't…" I interrupt the exchange. I need to try and stop this before it gets out of hand. Dragon might be out of line, but he is the club president, and you just can't talk to him like that.

Dragon waves me off, and leans on the table, looking at Skye intently.

"I'm an ass to anyone who thinks one of my brothers isn't good enough for them."

"I never once said that. Bull is an amazing person."

"Then why you making my boy jump through hoops?"

"Bull is a grown man, I doubt anyone could make him do anything he didn't want to do."

"You like my boy?"

"Jesus, Dragon. Let it go. Skye and I got this," I interject, because I'm about to step out of line even more than Skye, and I *know* what that means.

"Very much," Skye says, and when I turn to her, I notice

she's looking at *me* this time—not Dragon. Hell, that's enough to do something to a man.

"Then what's your deal?" Dragon prods, *yet again.*

"You have a child, right?"

"Dom, yeah."

"Then I'd lay odds that whatever you do in the future, you will go slow and worry about how your decisions will affect him. Or maybe I'm wrong. Will you just jump in with both feet and let him live with the consequences?"

"What happens if you decide to take a chance, Skye?"

Fuck! I hold my head down when Nicole asks her that. This is a fucking nightmare. I'm one step away from grabbing Skye and taking her the hell out of here.

"Then I will jump in with both feet and fight like hell to make it work."

Dragon, seems to consider her answer.

"You're mouthier than Bull's regular type."

"Since I've met some of his past playthings, I'll take that as a compliment."

"Playthings?" Dancer asks, and before he can even begin to think she's talking about Carrie, I answer.

"She works with that fucking bitch, Melissa."

"Fuck a duck, and you're still here with him?" Dance asks.

"Someone told me I need to live a little," Skye answers, and the tension inside of me lets go. I squeeze her side and kiss the top of her head.

"I think there's too much damn testosterone in here. Would you like to meet baby Dragon, Skye?" Nicole asks.

"I'd love too."

Nicole gets up and kisses Dragon quickly on the lips, but pulls away before he can grab her—like I know he wants to.

"He's just like big Dragon, but not as bitchy. Well except when it's dinner time."

"Woman!"

"Hush, sweetheart. You can spank me later."

"Always busting my balls," Dragon grumbles.

The women walk off, and I sit down. The prospect I elbowed earlier brings me a beer. I rarely drink now. But hell, after watching Dragon lay into Skye, I need one.

"You really think this chick is the one?" Dancer asks, but I can feel both his and Dragon's eyes on me.

"I know it," I say easily, taking a sip, and staring them head on. "Zero doubt."

Dancer nods. Dragon seems to be considering something and then sighs.

"She's got gumption. I'll give her that. And if she's still here after dealing with a club hanger-on as fucked up as Melissa, she has staying power."

"That bitch put a bug in her ear about the Twinkies, Drag. Even went so far as to call herself a member of the club," I tell him.

"I'll bring that fucking shit up at our next Church meeting. I'll let the boys know she's not allowed in the club from here out."

"Good. Hell, with the shit she keeps pulling, I'm surprised Skye will even talk to me."

"You're keeping her?"

"Absolutely. She's a hell of a woman," I answer honestly.

"I hope it works for you man, but if you keep her, you need to explain how things work. I can't have her disrespecting me again."

"I'll explain things to her once we get settled," I tell him, because in my eyes there is no *if.* There is nothing to consider. As far as I'm concerned, Skye and I are a done deal. I just need to make sure I give her every reason to hold on and keep trying.

Chapter 21

SKYE

I SURVIVED. THAT'S all I can think. Once I got through Dragon's unnerving interrogation, I had a really good time. It's definitely not what I expected. Though, Nicole did warn me it gets wild during parties. She pretty much confirmed everything Bull said. As well as, tell me things about Bull that I was starting to suspect, but still, it was nice having confirmation. She told me how he took care of her when everyone thought Dragon had died, and how he was always there to depend on. Later, I got to see him with Little Dom and that helped even more. The man who is slowly unraveling before my eyes is not the Bull I had painted in my mind.

The question remains, where do I go from here? I told Nicole if I jumped it would be with both feet and I would fight like hell to make it work. I meant that, and I want it....

"Skye?" I look up to notice that we've pulled in my driveway and the car is off. I didn't even realize we had stopped.

"Yeah?"

"You're awful quiet. Care to clue me in on what you're thinking?"

"Just going through everything that happened today."

"Doc, I know Dragon was rough on you, but he's just being a fucking busybody. He wouldn't..."

"He was worried about you. He and Nicole care a lot about you."

"Skye…"

"It's okay Bull, honestly. I really liked them. They're your family."

"They're the only family I've ever known," he says and I can see that. You can tell they are close.

"We don't really make sense, do we Bull?" I ask him, looking out of the passenger window at my house. Matty is somewhere inside with Blair and probably her husband. I have rounds tomorrow, my life is this tight little ball of organization and Bull...*Bull just doesn't really fit into any of it.*

"Not on paper, I guess Doc. But everywhere else, I think we make perfect sense."

"The house is full inside, or I'd invite you in," I tell him and I'm telling the truth. I don't really want him to leave just yet.

"I know, Doc. When's the next time you have off?"

"Who knows? Dr. Eldridge and Walter have been working overtime to make sure I'm miserable."

"I need to have a talk with Walter-boy again," he says and I sigh.

"No, you don't. I think you made a big enough mess the first time around. It'll die down eventually."

"Doc, that's not who I am. Someone or something bothers my woman, I fix it. End of the fucking story."

"Real life isn't solved that easily."

"It is for me, Doc."

"Let's just see if it gets better on its own. If it gets worse, I'll tell you."

Bull sighs. He doesn't answer. I take that as his agreement. Then, we're left in an awkward silence. And everything about it feels wrong.

I take a big breath and let it out slowly.

"Bull? I don't want this."

Chapter 22

BULL

I DON'T WANT *this…*

Her words slam into me, and damn, they hit me harder than any punch I've ever taken in my life. *She's mine.* I know I said I would walk away, but I didn't really think it would come to this. *Fuck!*

"Damn it, Doc, I know we come from different worlds, but…"

"No! I mean… I don't want us to be awkward with each other, and talking everything to death. I want to keep seeing you. I want you to spend time with me…with Matty."

Talk about a gamut of emotions—from one extreme to the other. She's definitely sent me into a tailspin here.

"So, we're going to do this? I ask her, because I need the words."

"I think we should."

"No backing out, Doc."

"No backing out. Where do we go from here?"

"Well, if your house wasn't full of people, and Matty wasn't going to be awake for hours, I would take you inside and fuck you hard."

She lets out an audible breath, it's shaky, and she shifts in her seat. "Yeah," she says, and it makes me feel good that she is definitely not happy about waiting. "That's probably not going to happen today."

"Soon though, Doc, because I'm hanging on by a thread here."

She turns those blue eyes on me and gives me a nervous smile, "Soon, Bull."

"I'm going to need a kiss to tide me over." I click the lever on the car seat and scoot it back as far as it will go. I adjust the steering wheel and then recline the back. "Come over here and get in my lap woman," I tell her, waiting to see if she will.

She looks at me, and then back to my lap, like I'm crazy. She shrugs, before unlatching her seat belt, and sliding next to me.

"Not good enough." I lift her so that she has a leg on each side of me, and we're looking straight at each other.

I swear I can feel the heat from her sweet little pussy, even through my jeans. I pull the edges of the long dress she's wearing even further up and rest my hands on each of her hips.

"Have I told you, Doc, that I like it when you wear dresses?"

"I don't think so."

"I fucking *love it* when you wear dresses," I tell her, and she smiles, looping her hands around the back of my neck.

She leans into me, kissing the side of my face, before whispering in my ear.

"I'll see what I can do about wearing them more often."

I've spent the last twenty-four hours worrying if I was going to have to give her up. Now that I know I'm not, I can't hold back. My fingers trace the small thin strip of lace that crosses each hip. I let my hand slide down her stomach to hold the soft silk of her panties. I move further down, pushing my finger against the material, using enough pressure so that her lips are pushed apart, and her hard little clit pulsates against the pad of my finger. The fabric between us is wet with her need. I push and slide the fabric around, using it to torture her clit, while hating it, because I don't like having it between us.

She whimpers my name, "Bull…"

"I'm going to make you come, Doc. Right here in the car, I'm going to make you come all over my hand, so that while we're apart you will have something to remember."

"Oh, God…"

I take my hand away, bringing it back to her hip. I loop my fingers into the soft lace on each side of her hips and pull. They snap, almost at the same time.

"I liked those panties."

"I'll buy you new ones."

"I can't believe after months of trying to run away from you, I'm letting you…"

"Letting me what, Doc?"

"You know!" she says, gasping, when I pull her torn underwear away. I put it in the pocket on the inside of my cut. "What are you going to do with those?" she asks, while rocking against my cock, which is now pushing against her heated opening.

"Wrap them around my cock while I jack off, remembering the way you looked when I finger fucked you and made you come."

"Bull…" she whispers, bearing down on me and shuddering in my arms, her eyes go hazy with lust.

"Tell me, Skye. Tell me how much you want me to fuck you."

"God, I do. It's been so long, Bull."

"I told you once before, Doc. I don't want to hear about anything that happened before me. As far as I'm concerned, I will be your first and I'm going to make sure it blows every other memory out of your mind. Now let me hear you beg me to fuck you."

"Please," she says, pushing harder against me and riding the hard ridge of my jean-covered cock.

"No. I want the words. Tell me you want my fingers in your pussy. Tell me you want me to fuck you. I want to hear those words."

"Why?" she cries when I pinch her hard nipple, for resisting.

"Because I want those dirty words falling from your lips right before I take them. Now say it, Skye."

"I want you…to put your fingers in me and…fuck me, Bull. God, make me come. I need to come so bad."

"Fuck yeah, I think I like this side of you, Doc."

"You're talking too much," she tells me, grinding on me again.

How long have I dreamed about this?

I push two fingers into her, and groan as they sink into that swollen, slick pussy. I want my dick in there so bad my balls are screaming at me. I want to march her in the house and tell everyone to get the fuck out. I need her stretched out on a bed where I can fuck her the rest of the night. Hell, when I finally get her in a bed, I may never let her out of it.

"Jesus, Doc, you feel good."

Her walls close in on my fingers, milking them. My cock fucking throbs, and I feel my pre-cum slowly glide down the head. *I need in her soon.* Maybe I shouldn't wait. Maybe I could fuck her right here in the car….*God knows I want to.* I pull my fingers out, groaning at the slick wet sound it makes when her pussy is forced to release them. I hit the lever on the side of my seat again. It takes some fumbling, but I finally connect and the back of my seat extends until it lies completely flat. I praise the car maker's ingenuity. I may hate cars and miss my bike, but right fucking now, I'm a fan for life.

"What…what are you doing?" Skye asks, her hair rumbled, and her skin flushed with desire.

"You're going to move up here and ride my face, Doc."

"We'll break the seat," she says, letting her self-consciousness close back in on her.

"I don't give a fuck. You have two choices. You ride my cock or my face. If you don't pick soon, I'll pick for you."

She watches me briefly, and I can see her indecision. She wants my dick as much as I want to give it to her. The only thing holding me back, is that when I have her, I will not be able to leave her afterwards. When I take her, I want to make sure I can love her all night long. Still, if she chooses my dick, I'm not stupid. I'll fuck her so hard and quick her head will spin.

Finally she makes her decision and part of me rejoices—*my balls throb in pain and curse me*. I'm scared to see what the fuckers look like at this point.

"This is crazy. We're going to break the seat," she mumbles, while she inches up my body. I slide down a little to make it easier. My hands bite into her thighs. I grab the dress at her back, and pull so it exposes her bare pussy to me. Sweet cream, thick and glossy, coats her lips and there is not a single hair in sight.

I flatten my tongue, licking just the outside of her lips, and when her taste hits me, I shudder in response. I push my tongue into her opening, and the tiny muscles in her pussy flutter at my entry. Cream drizzles from her, dripping into my mouth. I rake my tongue across her tender skin, trying to drink it all. I drink from her pussy, wanting…no *needing* more. My tongue swirls around her clit, mixing her desire against the hard pulsating little nub, as I suck it in my mouth. I latch on, torturing it, I can feel it pulsating, and she cries out when I slide a finger into her pussy. I bite gently on her clit, then use my tongue to pet the same spot, while sliding yet another finger in her. Her body jerks and twists above me. My other hand bites into her thigh, keeping her where I need her.

Now with two fingers in her pussy, I bend them so they scrape the top of her walls, while my tongue continues to work her clit. Her body clamps down on me, demanding everything I'm giving it. Her greedy pussy is grinding against my face, while she takes what she needs form me. I glance up and watch her as she rides. Her head is thrown back in pleasure, her hands are caressing her breasts, and her body is moving back and forth in the same rhythm my fingers are setting.

Damnation! I could come just from watching her take what she needs. My dick is throbbing about to explode, and I can feel my balls draw up with need. It's not happening though. When I unload for the first time, you can bet your ass, it will be inside this sweet heaven I'm feasting on.

"Bull…make me come please. Oh God honey, I'm so close."

I shouldn't have noticed, because I have my fingers deep inside of her, I have her taste all over my tongue and I have the best fucking fantastic show in the world happening above me, but I do.

Honey.

She called *me* honey. She's begging *me* for more. *Me.*

I've been close before, allowing myself to have feelings for another woman, but never in my fucking life have I felt anything close to what grabs hold of me right now.

Mine. Motherfucking-son-of-a-bitching, mine. I'm not giving her the fuck up. I'm not backing down, and I sure as hell am never fucking letting go.

Her softly spoken, *honey* is my undoing. I growl with ownership, with pride, *with complete fucking pride*. Then, I set off making her come all over my face. My fingers thrust in and out of her pussy hard and fast, while my other hand imprisons her thigh, not letting her lift away. She's my prisoner. Harder and faster I fuck her, curling my fingers up, keeping them closed on entry, and then stretching them apart when they dive deep inside of her. I let the tops of my fingers scrape against her walls, causing her whole body to jerk in reaction.

I bring her against my lips, rewarded as her breathing gets louder. She pants, while clamping down so tight on my face I could fucking smother in her juice. The fine tremors in her pussy increase and she convulses, sucking my fingers in so deep, my dick is jerking, demanding his turn. I suck her clit in my mouth one final time and bite down on the hard nub, giving her just a small spike, and that's all it takes.

I look up at the exact time she shatters. Her hands move up to the roof of the car and she braces herself, as her hips rock back and forth, grinding down, hard on me, and covering me in her cream. I lick her slowly, letting my tongue pet her swollen overworked cunt, until she rides out the storm I've created. With a final shudder she collapses against me and all I can think is I'll never have enough of Skye.

Never.

AW

SHE LET HIM defile her. In daylight with her son so close he could have seen what a whore his mother is. Does he mean so little to her? Do I? The times that we've spent together. The looks and touches we have shared. Can she ignore them so easily?

I've been letting things slide. Letting her discrepancies pile up because they seemed innocent enough. This can't be forgotten. She has stained her body. She has belittled us. *She must pay.*

I watch as she walks to her house. That Neanderthal watches every move she makes. Skye opens the door and her son runs out into her arms. She holds him close and places a kiss on his head. A kiss with the same lips she kissed *him* with. She holds her child close, *while she still smells of him.*

My decision is made. She was bad. She's taken it out of my hands. It saddens me, but I must bring her down. When she is at her lowest, that is the only time I can rebuild her. I will have to spend months cleansing her body.

It didn't have to be this hard. I was trying to be nice.

She caused this.

Chapter 23

BULL

"**Y**OU OFF TO that doctor chick's again?" Hawk calls out. Gunner is in on leave and they're enjoying the party tonight. Before Skye, I would have been right in the mix. The party is in full swing and a mixture of the single men from our crew, and a few of Skull's men, most notably Torch and Beast. Torch is presently getting his cock sucked on by the twins. My cock protests. He hasn't seen action in so long, the bastard hates me. I've even stopped yanking off to my own hand, because it got to where it just made me miss sex more. My damn dick has been permanently hard, since I got Skye off in the car two days ago.

"What doctor?"

Son of a bitch, I look over at the nurse from hell, Melissa. You can see the hate pouring off of her. She's been pissed at me since I called it quits. She's in Nailer's lap and it'd take an idiot not to see where that's going.

"None of your fucking business," I growl, though I'm sure she knows. She's just being a bitch. "Make sure you suit up man," I warn Nailer. I've not advertised the fact that the fucking gash gave me the clap, but I'd feel like an ass if I didn't warn him somehow. I need to talk to Dragon. He told me he was going to bar this bitch from coming back here.

"Always man!"

"Fuck you!" Melissa yells, and that's it. I was just going to wait until I talked to Dragon again, but I don't want this bitch in my club anymore. I march over to Nailer, yank her out of his lap, and pull her away.

"What the fuck are you doing? Let me go!" she bitches, pulling against my hold, but I don't let her go. Instead, I pull her to the front door.

"You been talking about the club to Skye."

"So?" she huffs.

"First, you are never to speak of shit that takes place in this club, but you not only did it, you did it to cause problems between me and her, and that fucking shit don't fly."

"If you're dating her, she knows all about us club girls anyways. Now, if you'll excuse me, I'm going to go inside, and get with a real man."

"Hey man, what's going on?" Nailer asks at the door, but I ignore him.

"That fucking shit right there can end too. You aren't part of this club, bitch. You ain't nothing but easy pussy. You think you can cause shit, and poison my woman against me? You think you can make yourself look big by saying you're one of ours? Fuck that shit. You're out of here. You don't get back through these motherfucking doors, and if one of my brothers see you, they'll kick you out on your ass."

"Fuck you! You couldn't wait to get your dick in me before that fancy whore of a doctor came along. Well, she opens her legs just like the fucking rest of us. She ain't special!"

"That's where you're wrong. Fuck, the only reason I ever touched you was for the fucking pills you pushed my way. If I hadn't been blown out of my mind, my dick would have never let my dick near you. Now get the fuck out of here, before I show you exactly what Savage MC does with people who think they can talk shit about us in public."

"You'll regret this, and your damned girlfriend will too. Just wait and see. I have connections. You made a big, freaking mistake thinking you could tell me what to do."

"The only fucking mistake I made, was messing with you in the first damned place. But Skye is my old lady. You want to pick a fight with her, you better fucking realize she has the club's protection, and I think you know what that means."

"Nailer! Tell him how…."

"You best get to walking," Nailer says slapping my shoulder and going back in—closing the front door.

I stand there, staring Melissa down. Her body is tight with anger and the hate is rolling off of her, but thankfully, she turns and walks off.

Fuck, I really must have hit rock bottom to ever deal with her ass. I need to get out of here. Being around a party these days makes my skin feel itchy. I can't handle it. There was a time I'd be high as a kite enjoying that shit. I don't think my brothers even noticed how far in the hole I had sunk. Well except, Crusher and Dani. He calls me pretty often to check on my ass. I miss the sad fuck, but the two of them are damned happy with Diesel's crew.

"Well that was exciting!" I look up when I hear Carrie's voice. "Wish I had pictures."

I can't help but laugh.

"Where you headed?" Dancer asks as they come to a stop in front of me. We all three turn and watch as Melissa's taillights disappear into the night.

Dancer pulls Carrie's back against him and wraps his arms around her, kissing the side of her neck. He isn't doing it to be mean. He's always touching her, holding her close. He's totally in love with his girl. It doesn't bother me now, like it once might have. All I can think is, I want my woman in my arms.

"Headed over to Skye's, and I'm running late." I damned anxious to get there too. Matty is spending the night with a friend, and this is the first night she's had off since meeting the club. Which hopefully means that after two days of reliving Skye coming as I finger her, tonight I finally get to fuck her until we both pass out.

"You think that bitch will be a problem?" Dance asks.

"Hell, I don't know. Probably."

"I thought Dragon blackballed her from the club?"

"He did. One of the prospects must have fucked up—we need to let him know."

"Will do. So this doctor? You're hung up pretty bad on her," Dance says with a cocky grin. Bastard, he's happier about it, than anyone. I don't mind it though. Hell, in his shoes, I would have kicked my ass for even talking to Carrie.

"Pretty bad," I agree. "And you two are keeping me from her, so I'll see you later."

"Do you care to come in and have a beer with us in Dragon's office? I'd like to talk to you about Jazz's christening."

Fuck. I don't want to, but they hit my weak spot. So, I follow them back in. I could almost laugh when Dancer keeps his body between the party and Carrie, until he gets her back into Dragon's office. Except I can see me doing that exact same thing with Skye. The thought makes me smile.

Chapter 24

MELISSA

THAT ASSHOLE THINKS he can make a fool of me? I have just as much right to be part of that club as some of them other bitches. I'm tired of trying to play nice. This is all that damned Skye's fault. I'm done rolling over. She has the doctor I'm fucking mooning after her, and everyone knows the Chief of Surgery is dying to fuck her. All of that, and she goes after Bull too? *I've had it.*

I don't think—I just drive out to her house. I figure I've only got about ten minutes, maybe less, before Bull gets here. Luckily, I'll hear his bike before he gets there. That will be the only warning I have, so I have to make sure to pay attention. I park my car about ten feet past her driveway. I pull it off to the side behind the guardrail. That way if Bull's bike's headlight shines out this way, he'll still never see it.

I fish around in my purse until I find my nail clippers. Then I climb over the fence and walk through Skye's yard. I try to stay in the shadows, away from the street light. I'm glad she doesn't have a dog. My heart is thrumming against my chest. I probably should have thought this through further, but fuck, I'm tired of being treated like scum. Bull wanted me all the time when he could use me. Then the good doctor waves her ass at him and bam....

I look at Skye's Volvo, and instantly wish I had paid more attention to my brother when he worked on cars. Brake lines have to be easy to find though, right? I crawl under her front of her car. I know where the brakes are, I've seen my brother put new pads on. I follow them till I find a line—*or at least what I hope is a line.*

I use my nail file—it takes six fucking times, but I finally stab a hole through it.

Fluid squirts on my chin and neck.

"Damn it!" I hiss, crawling out from under the car. I pull the tail of my shirt up to wipe my face and chin off. I can't stop a scream when a hand clamps down on my shoulder.

Oh fuck, fuck, *fuck*! How did I not hear Bull pull up?

AW

MY HAND BITES into the whore's shoulder. She screams, but I place my other hand over her mouth before much sound can escape. I jerk her around, keeping her screams muffled. Her eyes dilate with fear, her pupils expanding.

I feel myself harden, and I hate her for it! She's like every other whore, trying to tempt me with her body. She wants to soil me, and bring me to his knees. I take my hand away slowly, my eyes never leaving hers.

"What? What are you doing here? Oh my God, don't tell me she has you crawling up her ass too? Doesn't she have enough men chasing after her ass…?"

Her words end in a croak. I wrap my hands around her throat, applying pressure. I squeeze and she claws at my hands, digging her nails in and scraping my skin.

The metallic odor of blood hits me and I smile. Her eyes expand and I can see the small red vessels darken in her eyes. My smile broadens. She jerks and tries hopelessly to pull my hand away. Tears stream down from her eyes and I'm struck that finally Melissa has reached the beauty she's always longed for.

She's beautiful in death.

As her body sags lifelessly, I brace her against my body, and use one hand to twist her neck until I hear it snap. Then I let her fall to the ground. I pick up the small pair of clippers with the pointed nail file she had used—it fell when I grabbed her. It is only a testament to her stupidity now. I quickly jog to my car and return with my screw driver. In no time, I loosen the connectors that the brake lines in. The lines are rusty. If they hadn't been Melissa would have never made her small hole. Of course the small hole she made would have taken years to accomplish anything. Melissa always was an idiot.

Once my work is done, I pick her up and carry her away. I came to show Skye what happens when women lower themselves into the pits of sin. Melissa at least helped me with that. Excitement runs up my spine. The way everything is snapping into place is yet another sign, all working together to show me that Skye is the one. I just hope she learns her lesson.

Chapter 25

BULL

I MAKE IT to Skye's on autopilot. When I get there, the last thing I expect to find is the front door opened.

"Skye?" I call out, instantly concerned. I've been through too much shit with my brothers not to have fear run through me, when I see her door unlatched.

Nothing seems off as I look around the living room. "Skye?" I call out louder this time, she doesn't answer, but I hear her singing. I lock the door and follow the sound of her voice. I smile at the doorway to her master bath. She's singing in the shower. It's horribly off key, but I love it. While I listen to her singing about bringing sexy back, I can't help but admire the view of her body in the frosted glass door. She's washing her hair. Other than the color of her skin, and her general outline, I can't see much. It doesn't stop my dick from demanding we jump in the shower and join her. *I want to.* I should just do it and not worry about how she will react. I can't bring myself to be that person though. Besides, I'm pissed at her.

I ignore my dick and his demands and go into the kitchen. I order a pizza and turn on the television. Skye comes out a little later wearing a thick, pink fuzzy robe.

"Hey," she says smiling, and I turn the television off.

"Why would you get in the shower with the fucking door wide open, Doc?"

"What? You texted and said you were on your way."

"And I was, that doesn't mean you jump in the shower and leave your fucking door open for anyone to come in."

She takes a step back, and stops running the towel through her hair.

"Stop being grouchy. I couldn't have been in there more than a couple of minutes. I knew if I didn't leave the door cracked, you wouldn't come in. There was no way I could hear you from in there, so this was just easier..."

"Then you fucking wait until I get here to shower, or you text me and tell me where your spare key is. Or fuck, give me a fucking key. What you do *not do* woman, is leave your door opened, or fucking *unlocked*."

"Woman?"

"You heard me."

"I think you should go."

"Not hardly." I tell her, tossing the remote on the sofa. The doorbell rings and I get up to answer it, ignoring her.

"What are you doing?" She growls.

"Answering the door to get the pizza I ordered. Then, I might be nice enough to let you eat before I tan your hide."

"Tan my hide?"

"You heard me Doc," I tell her, yanking the door open. I give the guy some money and take the pizza back to the kitchen table, before coming back to the living room where Skye is still standing in shock.

"I don't want you here now," she grumbles.

"Too damned bad. Now, are you eating pizza or not?"

"You know I'm kind of rusty at this whole dating thing, but I'm pretty sure you're supposed to be nicer to the woman you're seeing."

"I'll be nice to you, later—in bed."

"Bull!"

"I'm only going to ask you one more time. Do you want pizza? If you keep arguing with me, I'll punish you for giving me lip in addition to putting yourself in danger."

"Punish me? You do realize I'm not a child right? That I'm a grown woman?"

"Believe me Doc, I am more than aware of that."

She blushes, and I know she gets my meaning.

"You should go."

"I told you that's not happening."

"You can't treat me like a child, Bull."

"Then you need to stop acting like one."

"Fine! I shouldn't have left the door open..."

"Or unlocked," I interrupt her.

"Or unlocked! You can bet your blueberry pancakes I'll lock you out from now on!"

"Blueberry pancakes?"

"I don't say bad words when I'm at home! I don't want Matty to hear them! *You know that!*"

"I know how to make you curse...maybe we need to revisit that *now* instead of later," I tell her and I'm not really kidding.

"You should be glad I don't curse, dang it! Because right now I really, *really* want to curse you until a fly wouldn't light on you."

"Do it," I dare her.

"I...oh shut up!" She grumbles, marching down the hall.

I'm going to punish her, but now it's become a mission to see how many filthy words I can get out of her mouth. I catch her just inside her bedroom. She tries to slam the door on me, but I push my foot against the door to stop her. I wrap my arm around her waist, bring her back hard against my chest, and lean down, whispering in her ear. "Are you getting pissy with me because I worry about you, Doc?"

"I'm pissy with you, because you're treating me like a child. You know, Bull, I got along fine before you came along. I don't need to be talked down to."

"Trust me, Doc. It's never occurred to me to treat you like a child."

"Then what was the flipping sermon for?"

"Flipping?" I laugh and kiss behind the shell of her ear where she has a birthmark. I lick it and suck it in my mouth. My dick leaks and jerks. God, I can't wait to fuck her.

"Let me go!" she grumbles, but I can see small bumps of excitement come alive along her neck—besides I'm not ready to let her go. *I'll never be ready to let her go.*

"I can't yet, Doc. You haven't learned your lesson."

She grows completely still against me.

"What lesson?"

"You're mine now, Skye," I tell her, I'm done going easy. Waiting for her *ends tonight.*

"What? I…Bull we've barely started seeing each other."

"Woman I've been chasing your ass for fucking months. It's a nice ass, don't get me wrong. But a man, especially *me*, doesn't put this much effort into something if he's not claiming it. *You're mine.*"

"Claiming it?"

I untie the belt of her robe. She doesn't fight me, so I count that as a yes. I lay my hand flat against her stomach, not moving it until she shows me some kind of sign. My tongue tastes the sweet skin of her neck, before I tease the side of her ear with my teeth. She tilts to the side to give me better access with a quiet moan.

"Claiming you. Every. Fucking. Inch. Of. You."

"Bull...I'm supposed to be mad at you," she says. My hand drifts against her bare pussy, I cup her heat, her hand reaches up, and her fingers bite into my neck. She pulls my head hard into her neck. I bite the tender area where her neck and shoulder meet, then brush away the sting with a kiss.

"You're already wet for me, Doc. Does my woman need to be fucked?"

"I do...but..."

"No buts woman," I growl, as my fingers part the lips of her pussy, and I stroke her clit. My balls are literally pulsing with need. I already know when I get inside of her, I won't last long. I decide the best thing to do is to give her a small taste now, because fuck when I get in her it's going to be one fucking fast ride. *I feel like I haven't come in years.*

"Give me your hand, Skye."

She turns slightly so she can see my face. I don't let her turn further, because my fingers are going to stay on her pussy. Hell, we've barely started, and she's so wet for me that I will sink up to my balls instantly. She watches as I maneuver her fingers and take them into my mouth. I suck them teasingly, letting my tongue wrap around them and play. When I release them they're wet and glowing from my attention.

"Now," I tell her, guiding her hand down to where mine already is—waiting. "Slide your fingers around your clit—just like you do when you make yourself come."

"I don't...well I mean I use my vibrator..."

"Good to know. We'll play with that later too."

"I...oh my..." she releases on a large breath as I slide my fingers inside her pussy.

"Tease your clit, baby."

She does as I ask, relaxing completely against me. Her

sweet cream drenches me, as I fuck her slow and easy.

"Bull..."

"Go with it baby. Play with your clit, while I finger fuck you," I tell her. I use my other hand to torment her breasts. Her hips start pushing against me, grinding that sweet ass against my cock. My balls are fucking screaming at me, but I don't care. *This is too good.* Getting Skye off, is better than any sex I've ever had in my life. "That's it. Grind into my hand. You're squeezing my fingers so tight, so fucking wet and tight. I can't wait to fuck you hard and feel you taking my cock into this tight juicy little cunt."

"Bull!" she calls out, and I roll her nipple in my fingers and pull it hard, while increasing the speed I'm fucking her with my hand. "I'm going...I feel it coming, Bull..." she tells me, her head thrown back in pleasure.

"That's it baby. Let me have it, Doc. Let me have all of it," I order.

Just when I feel her pussy begin to spasm, I pull my fingers out and then thrust them hard back inside her. That's just what she needs to throw her over the edge, because she clamps down on my hands tight and rides out her climax. I praise her, whispering in her ear.

"You're so fucking hot, Skye. I want you baby. I need you so much. I'm going to fuck you so hard, you won't be able to walk tomorrow."

"Honey, oh God it feels so good. You're so good," she whimpers.

I pet her and stroke her hair, letting her come down slowly. Besides, I want to touch her. I need to stay connected with her.

When her body finally stops quaking, she slumps against me, and I let my tongue lap up the fine sheen of perspiration that's on the back of her neck. I bring her hand to me, turning her so she can watch. I take the fingers she used to bring herself pleasure and suck them into my mouth. I make a show of it for her, but truthfully, I want every drop of her sweet cum.

"Now for lesson number two," I tell her once I release her fingers with a popping noise. Her eyes grow large—they should. *She has no idea just what I'm going to do to her tonight.*

Chapter 26

SKYE

THAT GOT OUT of control really quick. I'd be a hypocrite if I didn't admit that I enjoyed every minute of it. When he looks at me with that cocky look of his and tells me it's time for a lesson, my heart beats out of control. It's excited and fear of the unknown—all rolled into one. I've jumped into this thing with Bull, pretty quick. Really quick—even too quick, if you take into consideration how we met. *I can't help it.* I'm drawn to Bull and whatever he's going to give me, if it is half as good as I just got, I am more than ready for more.

"Lesson?" I ask him, wishing I could keep the nerves out of my voice.

"Lesson one you just had. I know exactly what you need and I'll always make sure you get it. Lesson two, Skye, is that you *do not* put yourself in danger."

"I told you it was just a few minutes," I defend. I know he's right. I normally would never leave my door unlocked, but I was so excited to see him tonight, and I wanted to refresh and put lotion all over my body…it was stupid, but I'd never admit that to him. I wanted to go the extra mile for him.

He pulls my robe the rest of the way apart. Considering what we've just done, I shouldn't be embarrassed, but I have the strongest urge to pull it back together. I manage to stop myself. I'm not a shy virgin. I've not been for a long time. It's just, whatever this is with Bull seems more intense. I feel…exposed in ways I never have before.

I try to still my nerves, and help, letting my robe fall to the floor.

"Woman, you fucking take my breath away," he growls, and the timbre of his voice sends little pulses of electricity through my body. My already drenched center, gets impossibly wetter.

This man is becoming precious to me. My eyes go to his large hand as he caresses the underside of my breast, and then follows the curve of my side to the flair of my hips. His touch is warm, slightly abrasive and intoxicating. The way he takes his time and his thumb pets my skin at the same time, makes my knees weak.

"Bull…"

"Shhh…I'm admiring the view."

"The view?" I murmur.

"It's not often a man gets to look at perfection, let alone claim it, Skye. I'm a lucky motherfucker. I'm going to savor the moment—just like I'm going to savor you."

Has anyone every talked to me like that? Has anyone ever made me feel special? I haven't felt like anything other than a mom in so long. Bull reminds me that I'm a woman and apparently to him, a beautiful one.

"Kiss me…" I beg because as good as this is, I need more.

His eyes had been watching his hand. At my plea, he looks up and there's this dark look in his eyes. It doesn't scare me. It just inflames me.

"In time, baby. Right now I need you to get on the bed on your hands and knees."

"But…"

"You'll like where we're going. Just trust me."

That's what I'm afraid of. I may like it too much. I nod, and do as he asks. My fingers grab into the covers and I try not to think about how exposed I am.

"Lower, Skye. Scoot your legs out so you get lower to the bed for me and stick your ass up high," he orders. His hand wraps around my hip, and he helps place me where he wants me. I've never felt small in my life, but Bull makes me feel small and delicate. It's an amazing thing since I've spent most of life being awkward and unsure.

"Such fucking perfection. Do you know why I was so upset you left the door unlocked, Skye?"

I don't answer. My heart is beating so hard, I couldn't find my voice right now if I tried.

"You put something I care about at risk," he says, and his hand comes down hard against my ass. The sensation of fire flaring on my skin spreads under his hand and I shudder from the burn. I don't object and before I even could, his hand comes down again. I whimper, and stretch my body through the pain.

"I care about you Skye. I live in a fucking dark world and you and Matthew bring me peace. Do you know how worried I got that something had happened to you?" he asks, delivering another slap. "What if it hadn't been me that found you? What if some stranger came in and took what you are giving me now? *What if he hurt you? What if he had killed you?* Do you know how that would have destroyed Matthew's life? *What it would have done to me?"* He asks his questions, while his hand comes down again and again, simultaneously.

With each blow my excitement increases. Liquid heat runs through me, and I know I'm soaked, needing him in ways I have never needed or wanted another. How does he know what I like so well? Is it coincidence? Does he know what a tight routine my life is, and how divine it is to turn that over to him? How I want him be in control, when it comes to this one aspect? Does he know how much it turns me on, to have him use my body without asking? To take what he wants? To be a *man*. God, I'm dying to have him inside of me. Dying for whatever he does next. Anticipation is pounding through my bloodstream, and I can hear my breathing turn ragged, as I wait. With his last blow, his touch changes. His hand caresses the skin, and I feel the press of his lips too. His hand strokes through the burn. It feels as if he is reassuring me—letting me know that he cares.

"Fuck, it's so hot watching as your soft, white, ass turns pink with the outline of my hand. You were made for me, weren't you, Skye?"

I want to answer him, but my body is on fire. Instead, I buck against his hand.

"Please, Bull…"

"I got you, sweetheart," he tells me. I hear the sound of his zipper, and the rustle of his clothes.

I look over my shoulder, he's naked and so breathtaking my arms quake—nearly giving out, unable to support me. He gives me that cocky grin of his when he reaches into his discarded pants pocket, then pulls out at least seven condoms connected and hanging down like a ribbon, promising a night of pleasure. My eyes grow large.

"I've got more in the other pocket," he promises, as he places them on the bed by my knee. I'm starting to wonder if I will survive tonight.

Chapter 27

BULL

I TRACE THE outline of my hand on her ass. *My print*—highlighted and welcomed. A show of my ownership—because I do own her. Every fucking bit of her. I slowly pet her from her ass to her pussy, dragging my fingers in her sweet juice and coating them. I tease her swollen clit and she groans out. That sound from her lips just might be the best thing I've heard in my life. I move my fingers back the same path, painting her in her own cream.

I repeat my actions over and over, getting closer to the rosette opening in her ass with each turn. She's fucking soaking my fingers, but the way she rocks back against me, searching for more, is what really makes my cock demand I stop playing. I can't seem to tear my eyes away from her ass. I plunge my fingers deep into her pussy again, and she absorbs them with a wet sucking sound. I let my fingers bite into the cheeks of her ass, pulling them apart, so the small hole is exposed. I take my coated fingers and paint her perfect opening, making it glossy. One finger slides easily into her ass, and she cries out. But instead of denying me, her ass relaxes and my finger pushes through the tight muscles.

"Bull!" again she cries, as she clamps down on my finger. I bend down closer to watch as she takes it and eventually I add another. Carefully I let my fingers gently fuck her, pulling them apart inside her tight hole. I can feel how they stretch the taunt muscles, making her body quake in response.

"Has anyone ever had this ass, Skye?" I ask her, even though a part of me screams, no. I don't want to think of any other fucker with my woman. *Ever.* But this...this I must know.

"No...never," she exhales, as another shockwave takes her. She's so close to exploding she'll come for days.

"Good. I'm going to take it soon. Take it and make you beg for more," I promise. I pull my fingers out and then push them back in. Once they pop through the ring again, I let my tongue dance along the opening, licking the fine creased skin, that is covered in her sweet juice. I let my tongue dance with my fingers pushing so the tip is barely in her ass, letting it flutter faster and faster, while applying more pressure against the entire area surrounding her opening. At the same time, I stretch out my fingers inside her again.

"Holy fucking hell! What are you doing to me?" she cries. I smile and count it as a small victory when she curses.

"Branding you," I tell her honestly. I want her so well fucked and sated, that she doesn't have the energy to even question who her man is.

"Then fuck me!" she growls and my dick jumps and my balls grow so tight it's painful. I look down to see pre-cum running down the head.

Damn who knew I had a wildcat? I should get mad when she orders me, but all I can do is grin. That seems to be all I ever do around Skye. She cries out when I take my fingers away and I want to cry with her. I'm too busy tearing open the condom and then pulling the latex over my throbbing dick.

I hate these motherfuckers, but I will use them until Skye

feels comfortable.

"Damn it, Bull hurry up!"

"What's wrong, Doc?" I tease her while I guide my cock along the seam of her pussy, letting her sweet honey cover the condom and letting the head of my cock tease her clit to the point she nearly rears up off the bed.

"I need you to fuck me!"

She growls the words at me, and she barely finishes before my hand wraps in her gorgeous, fiery hair and I yank her head back. I don't do it easy either, I want it to hurt—*just enough*. Her head jerks back, and her cry echoes in the room, as I guide my dick to her opening, and then, plunge in quickly—not stopping until my balls slap against her pussy.

"Bull!" she screams, drawing my name out. I don't move. After months of needing her, I take a moment to memorize everything about the way her pussy squeezes my cock, the way the muscles milk me and demand I move. I love the way her body looks right now, the control I have over her, and finally I take a minute to register that nothing else in my life has ever felt like this—or will ever feel like this again. She's every dream I've ever had, every fantasy I've ever imagined, all come true...and she's mine.

Those are the words that repeat in my head, as I slide out of her depths, only to push straight back in. Harder and harder I pound her body. "That's it baby. You take that fucking dick." I groan, reaching around to pull on her nipple. "Milk me and show me how bad you need to come."

"Fuck....me...fuck...fuck...fuck," she whimpers the words over and over, as her body struggles to keep up with my demands. I fuck her so hard the headboard is slamming against the wall. She'll be fucking lucky to walk normal tomorrow. Shit. I don't want her to be able to walk tomorrow. I brace my foot on the bed, shifting the angle of my cock. I grab her hip and yank her back into me at the same time I thrust inside. With that she explodes around my cock, as she lets out a cry that could shatter glass. Her muscles tighten and release, then tighten and suck me deeper, before releasing and repeating. I feel my balls tighten and then streams of cum shoot into the condom, and this time it's me who throws my head back and yells. *In motherfucking triumph.* But I only growl one word—and there's never been a more honest word spoken.

Mine.

Chapter 28

SKYE

"**H**EY DOC, ME and Matthew were starting to get worried about you."

"Hey Mom!" Matty chimes in, with a smile bigger than the state of Texas.

I stop at the front door, almost afraid I've come to the wrong house. I just pulled a fourteen hour shift and was trying to drum up the energy to fix dinner, do laundry and spend time with Matty. Then I walk into...*this*.

Bull and Matty are sitting in the floor, putting together a model car that Bull brought by yesterday. My son is almost as attached to Bull as I am. It worries me, but slowly I'm starting to believe that Bull means what he says. I'm keep letting fear hold me back, but we've only been dating for a little while. I worry these feelings I am having, are just too soon.

Then things like today happen. I come home to this, with Matty all smiles and...

"What's that smell?" I ask, at the same time my stomach starts rumbling.

"I made some chili. Are you hungry, Doc?" he asks, and it's a completely innocent question. But he looks at me, and all I can remember is the way his eyes look—right before he fucks me. My body vibrates with need.

"I'm starved," I tell him, and I'm not talking about the chili. I'm talking about Bull. *It's all about him.* I think my world is starting to revolve around him.

"I'll get you some then. Did you have a good day?"

"It was actually really good. I mean it started when this man gave me a ride to work on his bike, and it just kept getting better."

"No run-ins with Walter-boy or Melissa?" he asks, and I know he's worried.

He told me a little about the scene with Melissa at the club, and to be honest I've been worried about her reaction too. I haven't seen her though. She's been MIA for the last three days. The head of the nursing staff said she didn't give them any warning just left them a note on the hospital administrator's desk that a family emergency came up and she was leaving the state.

I relay that information to Bull and he gets a puzzled look on his face.

"What?" I ask.

"Just didn't figure she'd give up that easily. She was really mad. Did Judy mind giving you a ride home?"

"Me either, but I'm not going to complain about it. And no, she's been really down since the house fire. Do you know they're having trouble getting the insurance to pay?"

"Why's that?"

"Apparently the Fire Marshal's report came back and they're saying it looks like the fire was purposely set."

"You're kidding?"

"Nope and since Judy and Tony were upside down on their mortgage, the insurance agent is being an ass."

"Da......darn it," he says with a wink. "Maybe the club could help them out?"

"She's got a meeting with the insurance company tomorrow, which means no bike ride tomorrow morning—as fun as it was."

"Does this mean I'm staying again tonight?" he asks in surprise.

"I was hoping you would. But sadly, I will drive my boring old Volvo, to work," I tell him, trying to play down the nervous flutter in my stomach. The truth is...*I don't want him to leave.*

"Jesus, I can't believe I'm dating a woman who drives a Volvo."

I stick my tongue out at him.

Bull laughs, before looking at Matty. "Okay, sport. Let's stop for the night and get your Mama some food."

"Aw! Man!"

Bull reaches over and ruffles Matty's hair, and my heart flips over inside my chest.

"We can finish up tomorrow, buddy."

"Now, go love on your mom," he tells him and I fall for him, a little more.

Matty comes and hugs me and I hold him close, before letting him go. There's times he rebels from being mom's baby. Then there are times like now, when he reminds me of when he was three and I was his world.

I talk with my son while Bull warms up my food. I ask Matty how his sleepover went and smile as he tells me about all of the video games they played. It's a big hint as to what he wants for Christmas, so I make a note somewhere inside my tired brain. Matty's spent the day with Bull. He volunteered to be here today when Matty got off the bus. I worried how he would explain it to Matty. Apparently he told Matty he wanted to spend time with his favorite buddy. Matty's chest puffs out in pride, when he tells me that. I look over his head at Bull, and he winks at me. I know I'm already half way in love with him. He comes back in with a tray that's loaded with a drink, a bowl of chili and some crackers.

"Wow, I think you might be trying to spoil me, Mr. Kane."

"You never know, Doc.

"Hey, Mom? I'm going to go play video games. I'm supposed to do an online battle with Greg."

"Greg?" I ask, because that's a new name.

"He's a new guy at my school, just like me. I just met him today. He's really cool."

"Okay. Have fun. I'll be in before bedtime to check on you."

"He's a good kid," Bull says, when he leaves.

"He is, he's growing too fast. I didn't know you could cook," I tell him, to distract my thoughts, the thought of Matty growing up and outgrowing me is a constant concern. It's a worry that's only gotten worse, since I don't have a lot of time with him right now.

"There's a lot of things you don't know about me, Doc."

"Such as?"

"Sweetheart, I can't give away all my secrets. I have to tempt you with them slowly," he jokes.

"Is that what you're doing?" I ask leaning against the back of the couch, feeling completely relaxed.

"Unleashing my awesomeness a little at a time to get you addicted? Absolutely," he says going down on his knees in front of me. He takes my shoes off, and then picks one foot up, tenderly massaging it.

"God, that feels better than sex," I moan.

"Fucking hell, I must be doing something wrong," he jokes, and I laugh as a yawn overtakes me. Bull takes my tray, and sets it on the coffee table, before continuing with his massage, concentrating on the balls of my feet.

I've almost dozed off, when the doorbell rings. I jerk and yawn again, but before I can get up, Bull waves me off.

"I got it, Doc," he says, already going to the door.

I'm close to being out again when Bull comes back. He's holding a white envelope, the kind you get with a greeting card, and reaches it to me.

"No one was there, but they slid this under the storm door," he says, handing it to me, before returning to work on my foot.

"That's weird," I say, looking at the envelope. It's addressed Dr. Skye Walker. That's it, no further writing.

"I thought so. It better not be another man trying to make a move on you."

I shake my head, because he's being foolish. It's nice he thinks I'm someone other men would notice. I've never had a self-confidence issue—it's just really nice to feel valued. I take the envelope with heavy eyes. It's going to take all I have to stay awake to kiss Matty goodnight.

I yawn, then grip the card. I look at Bull on impulse and reach down to kiss him quickly on the lips.

"I'm pretty sure I'm ruined for other men after last night," I tell him, not even caring that I'm blushing.

"Damn straight," he says, coming up to sit beside me. He takes me in his arms and kisses the side of my neck. "Could you feel me when you walked today, Doc? Did you feel empty?"

His wicked words send goosebumps over my skin, and I'm instantly aching for him. He was right last night. *He did brand me.*

"If I say yes, will you do something about it?" My tired

body is instantly ready for him.

"Absolutely, sweetheart."

"Then, yes times infinity," I tell him, as I open the envelope. I pull out a folded, thick piece of paper inside. It's not a card as I thought. Just a note, that's folded in half. I recognize the handwriting immediately.

Every sin must have a just recompense. You made me do it.
—AW

Chapter 29

SKYE

"**W**ILL YOU QUIT cursing?"

"Do you not get that some sick fuck is out there toying with you! This is the wrong fucking time for Dragon and Dance to be gone!"

"You said they went to spend Thanksgiving with Crusher and Dani and to celebrate them adopting a little boy. Will you relax? It's probably just some kid trying to scare me, or playing a very sick joke."

"You're being naïve, Doc. There are some twisted people out there, and I'm not sitting around on my ass while they target my woman. Fucking hell! Why didn't you tell me, you've been getting these notes?"

He's been going on like that for the last hour. I got Matty in bed and he called his club, then yelled and growled. He threw a pillow across the room, cursed some more, then called the club again. *Rinse and repeat, even.*

All this was kind of sexy for the first thirty minutes. The last thirty however, it has become annoying. When he picks up the phone to talk to Freak—*yet again*, I've decided I've had enough. I get up, and walk to the door that leads into the hallway. He's not even paying attention to me. I could be in California right now for all he knows. I mean, I know I've had a long day at work, still, shouldn't I be able to get my man's attention when I leave a damn room? I pull my shirt over my head and throw it down. Next, I pull off my scrubs, and then kick them out of the way. I might have kicked them a little harder than I needed to, because they land against a picture on the coffee table. The frame falls and slams on the coffee table with a loud '*thunk.*'

"Yeah, Freak. I want a prospect here watching over the property. Until we determine what this is, we need to treat it as serious. I'll be here the majority of the time, but I can't be here 24/7 I need to make sure my...." he stops mid-sentence, jerking his head up at the sound. "Skye?"

"I'll be in the bedroom if you're interested," I tell him, unlatching my bra and throwing it at him. I count it as a win, when it lands on his head and then slides down. He grabs the bright white cups with his free hand and tightens his hand on it. I make sure he gets a good view of my chest, then shimmy out of my panties, throwing them to the side. When I'm standing in the room completely naked, I stare at him, daring him to do something.

"Bedroom, Skye. I want you by the bed on your knees," he growls and chills run over my body. I think I've won. So I smile in agreement and head towards the bedroom.

"Freak man, I'm going to have to go...." I hear him in the background, so I pick up my pace, practically running to my room.

I kneel down by the bed, anticipation is running through my system. All it took was his order and my nipples pebbled like hard stones. Heat swamps my system, and desire coats the inside of my thighs. This man has my body on fire and he hasn't even touched me.

"Skye this isn't some damn joke. Some asshole has targeted

you here," he growls.

He'd be more convincing if he wasn't undressing. I guess I should be more worried. But really, this has been going on for a while now and nothing has really happened. If the police or hospital security were more concerned, maybe I would be too. They're not, so I can't bring myself to be. Instead my eyes are glued to this amazing man in front of me.

His body is like a work of art. He's tall and hard chiseled perfection. His dark skin calls to me. I love the way the light caresses it. I want to follow it with my tongue. For so long, I ignored anything that made me feel like a woman. Bull not only brings that back to life, with him everything is more intense that it ever was with anyone else. I lick my lips as he palms his hard cock and strokes it. Moisture gathers on the tip and I instinctively lean towards him.

"See something you want, Doc?"

Nervous butterflies flutter in my stomach. *I do.* I absolutely do. I worry for a second, but he's clean now. I've seen the reports and I've been imagining his taste for days.

"Bull, please."

He sits on the bed and I lean up, bracing myself on his knees, thinking *finally*—I'm going to get what I want.

"Don't touch me, Skye. Sit back down," he barks. I look up at him confused, but I do it. *I do it automatically.* I don't even think to argue with him.

His hand holds his balls, rolling them, and then he gives his cock one *long* stroke. I can't stop the whimper that breaks free at the sight.

"Bull, please."

"You see something you want, Doc?" he asks, and he tugs hard on his dick so the tip is almost at my mouth and I think he's going to give it to me. I want to stretch to get it, but I'm afraid he'll stop after his last reprimand. My tongue though, comes out and curls, silently begging. At the last minute he points the tip down and I feel his heated pre-cum caress just under my collar bone. I wait for more, but instead he reaches beside him and produces a bottle of lotion. I hadn't seen him grab it, I was too engrossed in his body. It's my vanilla and sugar lotion that I use all the time. He looks at the bottle with a leer. "Have I ever told you Doc, how much I love the way you smell? I dream of it. I've jerked off to it a hundred times. It reminds me of sugar cookies and that only makes me want to eat you up."

"Fuck, yes…" I moan, purposely giving him the word he loves to hear out of my mouth the most.

"Hold them perfect tits out for me, Doc and get up on your knees. *Now.*"

I do as he orders. When he commands me in that tone, my whole body convulses in need. He holds the bottle over me and a thick creamy strand creeps out, catches the side of my breast and then runs slowly down the deep valley I've created. He makes sure to do that several more times, my body shivers from the mixture of the cold lotion and the way I'm needing him.

"Move over here woman and get between my knees, then wrap them tits around my cock."

Who knew I could get so turned on by this? I do as he tells me, loving the way his dick lays against my skin, so big and warm. My eyes trace the veins, and the way his pre-cum already has him slick, before I envelope him in my breasts. I never really understood why men went crazy, because I had larger breasts, but now I'm thankful, because they wrap his cock tight, and I hold him into my body. He uses my shoulders to guide me, and shows me the motion he wants. Slowly, I follow his lead, letting his strong, hard member tunnel through. At the end of each thrust the tip of his dick pokes out.

My eyes are drawn to Bull. His gaze is intense, watching as he fucks my breasts. Every muscle on his face is tight—so rigid and precise. I'm dying to see him lose control. Make him go over the edge, like he makes me. With that in mind, I lick the tip of his cock every time it peeks through. I flatten my tongue and gather the pre-cum from the tip. When the salty liquid hits detonates on my taste-buds, I moan.

Bull's uncircumcised and while the foreskin is covered with a mixture of him and the lotion, the head of his cock is all him and it's delicious. When my tongue licks his head, his body shakes. I look up to see his scorching gaze on me. His hands overlap mine as he grabs my breasts. His thrusts get firmer, more intense, jarring my whole body and I love every minute of it.

"Did you like the way I taste, Doc?" he asks, and his voice is guttural, animal-like in nature, his eyes are glued to my chest and the way my tongue licks the crevice of his head, every time he finishes a thrust to expose it.

"Yes, honey. I want more. I need to be covered in you," I tell him and I don't know where the words come from, but I know *I want it.*

My words seem to be exactly what he wants, he tunnels faster and I can see his balls literally pulse. He lets go of my breasts to pull his dick out from the valley we created. He strokes himself. Once…twice and then jets of creamy, white cum bursts forth and lands on my breasts, stomach, my thighs, and then across my chin and lips. When he finally finishes giving it all to me, a giant shudder rakes through his body. This time when he looks at me, he's still intent, but gone is the cocky Bull that normally comes out to play. In his place is a man who looks as if he is going to eat me alive. *The thought alone is thrilling.* I lick the stream of cum that landed on my lips, using my finger to gather it off my chin too. I'm doing it to further tempt him, to tease him—because I can.

He stands and then picks me up in his arms without a word.

"Wait. Where are we going?" I ask, holding onto his shoulder and neck.

"We're going to shower. Then, after I clean you up, I'm going to eat your pussy until you beg me to stop, and then I'm going to fuck you against the wall."

His words thrill me and just to show my approval I bite the tendon that runs on the side of his neck before telling him the only word my brain can seem to form.

"Hurry."

Chapter 30

BULL

I RUB THE area above my left eye. The headaches have been getting better, but I can feel one forming. It pisses me off. After the workout that Skye just gave me, and the peace I feel, the last thing I want is another of these damned headaches. They vary in levels, but some of these fuckers can be blinding in pain. I've tried to keep the really bad ones hid from Skye. It shouldn't make me feel weak, but it does. It's worse now, because she needs me to be strong. She might not believe this threat is credible, but something in the pit of my stomach says it is. Which means, Skye needs a strong man, ready and able to defend her.

"Headache?" her sweet voice asks me. She's sleepy and there's a huskiness in her tone that I could easily listen to for the rest of my life.

"A small one," I curve into her body, then turn her. I don't want her to see me if the pain worsens. I kiss her shoulder, and I'm rewarded when she puts her hand over mine at her waist, and lets her fingers stroke gently against mine.

"I like this the most," she says.

"What's that, Doc?" I ask her.

"You holding me, feeling you surround me, and hearing your voice when I'm tired—all of it. When I think of us, this is what comes to mind the most."

Her answer does funny things to me. No one has been proud of me like Skye is. At least none I can remember. *None that mattered.* Maybe that's why my voice is so thick with emotion when I answer. It's an unusual feeling.

"Us, Doc? You better watch it, you're starting to sound like you want to keep me around."

Skye turns her head, to look over her shoulder at me. A man could die happy when she looks at him like that.

"I never want to let you go."

My hand goes to the side of her neck, to hold her in place. My lips come down on hers and our kiss is a promise. A promise that fills every part inside of me. I'm not going anywhere. I knew from the moment I saw her that she was my future. Every minute I get with her, I'm more convinced.

She turns on her back and our kiss deepens. She's like aged scotch, going straight to my head. My hand trails down over her breast and stomach and that's when it happens. Pain so intense that it flashes and hits me right behind my eyes. It's like someone takes a red-hot poker and stabs them repeatedly. I want to keep it quiet, not to let her see, but when it happens all at once like this, I can't prepare. I groan, and my eyes clench shut, then I fall back on the bed.

Skye leans over me and her hand goes to my forehead. Even with the pain, her touch feels good. *I just can't enjoy it.*

"Bull? Tell me what's wrong. Is it your head?"

I hear her questions, but I can't respond. All I can do is grunt, "Fuck."

"Oh God, honey," I hear her, and a minute later she's moves to crouch beside me. She's pushing on my shoulder, trying to turn me on my side. I go along with it, because I'm hurting so bad, I don't much give a fuck. This is probably the worst one I've had since we've started seeing each other. There's no way to keep it hid, like I have the others. Skye tilts my head forward, and then her hands are at the base of my skull. She presses hard there, and keeps the same pressure, but pushes upwards in a circular motion. Slowly it eases the pain. Not a lot, but it's not as blinding. "Any better?" she whispers near my ear. I hear it, but barely. The roaring of my blood and the beating of my heart echoes in my ears.

"Little." I can only manage one word. She clasps between my thumb and index finger. She moves her hand up to thickest area, and pinches—applying pressure. After a little bit, she switches hands. Slowly the pain lessens. It's still there, but a dull roar compared to what it had been. "What are you doing?"

"Using pressure points to ease your pain. We need to get you back to a neurologist."

"I've been to the doctors Skye. They can't find a physical trigger. Which pisses me off, this isn't in my mind."

She moves situating herself behind me, maneuvering so I'm resting against her, in between her legs. My back is against her stomach and my head is on her chest. She tilts me to reach the base of my neck, and begins massaging there.

"Of course it's not. I read a little bit about the trauma that you suffered in your hospital file. Do you still have the tremors too?"

"Well fuck, Doc. What's the point of keeping shit from you, if you have already seen everything?"

"Gee, Bull. I don't know. A better question might be, why in the world would you try to hide this from me?"

"I'm not weak, Skye."

"I never thought you were. Though, I'm starting to wonder how smart you are if you think I could ever view you as weak. Now, sit up for a second, and let me get you some medicine…"

"No pills, Doc."

"Bull…"

"I'm not taking no goddamn pills."

Her movements halt abruptly, she takes a deep breath and lets it out.

"Now that I have you Skye, I'm not taking a chance on anything that might make me lose you. *No pills*."

"Bull? What does that even mean?"

"I saw you and the minute you stood up to me, something clicked. I knew you were it. I wasn't about to touch that stuff again when I had my future staring at me."

"Oh. My. God."

"No pills, Doc. I'm not putting that in jeopardy."

"It's Ibuprofen, and a very mild dose, and *your future*? Do you know how crazy that sounds? You didn't even *know* me! Heck-fire! You don't even know me now! I could be a serial killer! Bull, that's not even sane and it's a piss poor reason for being sober. You can't pin your reason for staying sober on another person. That's just doomed for failure."

"Who says? It's a damned good reason for me. And I do know you. I know everything about you."

"No you don't, we just started dating, Bull, seriously…"

"I know you love the smell of coffee, but can't stand the taste. I know you take two hour long bubble baths even when you can barely stay awake, because it helps you unwind. I know your favorite food is Chicken Marsala, you only drink water with a twist of lemon on the side, but when you've had a really bad day, you will drink red wine. I know you love foot massages while you're watching silly Christmas movies on television, even though you say you don't like television. I know you hate the taste of spinach but love the dip made from it. I know you never talk to your parents and that they cut you off when you became pregnant with Matthew. I know you will come up with the craziest words to use instead of curse words, because you don't want to be a bad influence on Matthew. I know you love chocolate ice cream, but hate chocolate pudding. I know...."

"Okay, okay. Stop it already. I get it. You take really good notes when I talk."

"I'm not taking notes, Skye. You're important to me. Everything you are, and everything you do fascinates me. I'm not taking notes. I'm learning about the woman I love, because it brings me joy."

"Dang it, Bull! Do not make me cry. I'm going to get up and get you some ibuprofen. It's not addictive and hopefully it will stave off the majority of the pain," she says, patting my back, "lean up and let me out of here."

I don't want to. I don't want to let her leave. I like this connection with her. I do it, but as she stands up, I grab her hand and pull her so her lips are near mine. I look in her eyes. They punch me in the gut, just like they have from the beginning.

"I love you, Doc."

She doesn't answer, like I hoped, but she leans in and gives me her mouth. My tongue leisurely invades her mouth, taking time to taste her, and relearn everything about her, from the flavor, the texture, and hidden areas. Her tongue mates with mine, just as slow, just as relaxed, and somehow, it draws a deeper response between us than has been there before.

When we break apart her forehead rests on mine, her fingers are caressing each side of my neck.

"You aren't why I'm sober, Skye. You're the reason I want to be a better person. The reason I want to be a man that deserves you," I tell her, letting my hands get lost in her hair.

"You're the best man I've ever met, Bull. If I didn't believe that completely, I would never trust you with Matty, because he's the most important thing in my life."

I take in her words and let her leave me. Our eyes stay connected, because she backs away from me. I think it might be happiness I see in her. I can't help but return her smile—even through the pain.

"There's something you don't know about me, Bull," she says before she leaves the room.

I don't want to tell her she's wrong, but I'm pretty sure I know all things Skye.

"What's that, Doc?" I ask, just to humor her.

"When you smile? I feel like I've just won the lottery."

Damn. That's all I can think. *Damn.*

"I'll be sure to do that more," I tell her.

"That'd be appreciated, heck I might even reward you."

I do the only thing I can...I smile bigger.

Chapter 31

SKYE

I DEFINITELY MISS riding on the back of Bull's bike this morning. Even though the temperatures are cool this time of year, there's something amazing about holding onto him, while the wind whips through my hair. Plus, you can feel the joy radiate from Bull. Thinking of Bull makes my heart speed up. I'm in love with him. I haven't told him and I'm mad at myself because I haven't. I'm letting fear hold me back, and that's not fair to me or Bull.

I left Bull sleeping this morning. He'll be mad, I know—especially after the note from my friendly-neighborhood-stalker. But, he was in so much pain last night, and it was almost three this morning before he fell back asleep. I sure wasn't going to wake him up at four and tell him I had to leave to meet with my chief of staff in some emergency meeting. Walter texted. He asked me to come in for a meeting, before my rounds. He wouldn't explain why, so I'm worried. If I had to explain all that to Bull, he would have demanded I wait for him, and then I'm pretty sure he would have insisted on being present at the meeting. Sneaking out was my best option. I sent a text to Blair, who gets up at four thirty every morning anyways. I told her I was going in early and that Bull was with Matty right now, but she would might need to be on standby because Matty's holiday break at school starts today. I owe Blair so much and she barely lets me pay her.

I'm driving down the road and my brake light comes on. I want to groan out in frustration. This damn car just cost me two hundred dollars in repairs last week. I rub the tension at the back of my neck and pray it's nothing serious. My Christmas fund is going to be awful tight if it's something major. Matty wants a bike and I need to make sure he gets one, because he hardly ever asks for things.

I come to the stop sign at the end of my street and the car comes to a stop okay—but the pedal goes all the way to the floor, before it finally stops. *Damn.* I don't know much about cars, I was hoping the light meant I needed new pads or something. But now, I'm starting to worry it is low on fluid or something. That was supposed to have been checked at the last service.

I decide to drive extra slow, *just in case.* Dr. Walter can just be pissed if I'm late. I listen to the music on the radio, while thinking over my night with Bull. Who knew life with a biker could be so…normal. Well, *fucking hot,* but normal. I'm grinning like a loon as I start down old Crawford Mountain. I came this route without thinking. There's a second way to get to the hospital, it's just that this one is closer. The bad part is, it winds and twists in '*s*' shaped curves. They are so steep, that sometimes make you think you are passing yourself. I usually come this way, but if I had thought about it, I wouldn't have— especially with my brakes acting up. I'm a little worried, but I can always gear the car down into a lower gear, and that combined with my brakes should be enough to make it safe.

My cell phone rings and I pick it up, glancing at the number. *Great.* He woke up early.

"Hello?" I answer, trying to interject cheerfulness into my

voice.

"Doc, where the fuck are you?"

"I'm headed to work, honey." I tell him and I'm distracted by his anger. His anger irritates me. I was trying to do something nice for the dumbass. Besides, I'm a grown woman!

"Damn it, Doc! You told me you didn't have to go in until six this morning. It's barely five!"

I take a deep breath as I top the hill, and try to remember he's only being an ass because he cares about me. *He said he loved me.* That thought feels me with warmth.

"Walter called and asked me to come in before rounds for a meeting."

"I bet that sorry sack of shit wants a meeting. Why in the fuck didn't you wake me, Doc?"

"You had barely slept. I'm sure it's nothing, and I'm perfectly safe."

"You weren't safe when he tried to force himself on you, and did you forget about the fucking notes?"

"Bull, for gods-sake, I'm going to be in public at the hospital, I'll be fine."

"And the fucking notes?"

"Will you give it a rest? I'm sorry I even told you about them. If the police aren't worried about them, I don't know why you should be!" I yell back, upset with him, and that's bad because I forgot two very important things. I didn't gear down when I started going downhill. That might not have been horrible in and of itself, but the more agitated I get, the more my foot presses on the accelerator. I'm going much faster than I do normally, let alone when I'm worried about my brakes.

"The police are morons and I'm worried, because someone has been targeting my woman! Damn it, Skye! You better call me the minute you get to the hospital, and make sure you tell me what that fuckwad wanted. I have to go meet with Freak this morning, but I'll be…"

"Bull!" I stop him, because this time when I press the brake pedal nothing happens. Instead of slowing down, the car picks up speed.

"I'm sorry, Doc. I shouldn't have yelled. It's just I love…"

"Bull! My brakes aren't working!"

"What? What do you mean? Where are you?"

"I mean, I'm pumping the pedal and nothing happens! I just keep picking up speed!"

"Fuck, where are you Skye?"

"Coming down Crawford," I tell him, fear thick in my voice. I can feel the tears spilling from my eyes. I ignore them, trying to think of what to do. I'm a damned medical school graduate. I can do this. I hold human hearts in my hand while they're beating for Christ's sake.

"Fuck! Okay sweetheart, press hard on the brake pedal, does anything happen?"

"No! *That's what I'm trying to tell you!*"

"I need you to lift the lever for your emergency brake, Skye. Do it slowly, but get it up all the way."

Emergency brake. Why the hell didn't I think of that? I do as he says. I don't know what I expected. On television when someone does this, they usually fishtail in some kind of cool smoking doughnut, parking lot stunt. I've got the steering wheel gripped tight, waiting for that. *It never happens.*

"Why the fuck isn't it happening?" I cry out.

"Skye? What's going on?" Bull asks, and I don't know if it's just because I'm terrified, or if he is but, all I can hear is *you're going to die,* in his voice.

"Nothing! Bull! Why did nothing happen?"

"It had to slow down some, sweetheart. Now, I need you

to gear down into low gear. Can you do that?"

He's talking so cool and calm, and that should reassure me, but right now it doesn't. Still, I do what he tells me. My speedometer at one time read eighty, but now I'm in the curviest part of the hill. I do what he says, and notice my speed is down to sixty now. The hand on my RPM dial is way in the red. I decide I don't care if I do blow up my car—I may never drive again. My wheels screech as I slide sideways around a steep curve. My speed is now fifty-five and that's great! *It would be awesome*—except I'm not on an open road. No, I'm halfway down the mountain and going into the largest switchback curve of them all. My car slides again. Half of it goes air born when I cut the wheel too deep. My cellphone goes flying through the air, as I use both hands on the steering wheel, trying to get it back under control.

"Skye, sweetheart you have to talk to me."

I hear Bull's voice from somewhere in the car. I know he can't hear me, and I don't know where the phone is, plus the squealing of my tires is deafening. A horn blows, adding to the noise, because just as I do a one-eighty spin in the curve, another car is coming in the opposite lane, on the other side of the road. They are going slow, and they do their best to steer their car out of my path, but it's no use. I'm going too fast, my car is too out of control. I'm sideways and taking up entirely too much road.

"I love you, Bull!" I tell him, uselessly. Then, there is the screaming sound of metal against metal, as my car collides with the other. The air bag explodes, my head is thrown backwards...and then...*blackness.*

Chapter 32

BULL

I F I LIVE to be a hundred and one, I never in my lifetime want to relive those last few moments on the phone with Skye. Jesus fucking Christ, my body is still shaking a day later. She had her seat belt on thank God, and somehow— *miraculously,* she came out with just a mild concussion, some cuts, a few stitches and bruised ribs. The paramedics and medical staff were all amazed, and I guess I need to start praying more, because the way I look at it, I owe the big guy upstairs for still having Skye in my life. She lost consciousness for a little while, but she came through and was able to talk to me and Matty last night, before she went back out. I stayed with her. I had Blair and her man take Matty with them, but I put two prospects outside their home. I'm not taking any chances from here on out. I'm going to find who this mother-fucker is, and when I do, I'm going to tear them a part piece by piece.

I called Dragon, and instead of staying with Crusher until after Christmas, they're all coming back after Thanksgiving. I hated asking, but I need my brothers around me. I need to find out who this motherfucker is and get rid of them. I had thought it was Melissa, but I don't think she's dumb enough to try this stunt. Plus, I think my calling her out for talking about the Savage MC scared her, because the bitch has disappeared. Now that Skye has told me about all of the notes, I'm starting to think some man has her in his sights. The problem is, he is definitely a few bricks shy of a full load.

"Hey you," I jerk my head up, and lock eyes with Skye. Her poor face is bruised, scraped, and she has a hell of a cut on the side of her forehead. It took six stitches to sew it up. She's never been more beautiful to me, though.

"Hey, Doc," I tell her, my voice hoarse. I squeeze her hand and she tightens her fingers against mine briefly.

"You been here all night?"

"I'm not leaving you, Doc."

"You should have gone home to rest. You're going to bring on another one of those headaches."

"I'll sleep when I get you home in my bed," I tell her, and I'm not kidding. There's no way I will be able to sleep, until she's with me.

"When will that be?"

"Well I see you've decided to wake up and join the world."

I look up and the doctor who has been taking care of Skye comes through the door.

"Hey, Scott," Skye says, with a genuine smile and I try to ignore the hint of jealousy that I feel.

"Hey yourself. I didn't realize you were into fast cars. It's always the quiet ones you have to look out for."

I grit my teeth to keep from telling him to let go of her hand. It bothers me, even if he is just taking her pulse.

"When do I get out of here?" Skye asks the doctor. My hand shakes with the need to pull his hand away from her chest, as he uses his stethoscope. He doesn't know how close he's coming to losing that fucking hand.

I hear a giggle. Skye is watching me. She knows what's

going on in my head, and she's shaking her head. I just shrug, because hell—*I am who I am.*

"If all your test results come back okay, you can go home this evening."

"Thank God! And work?"

"No fucking way!" I interrupt.

"Ignore him, he gets grumpy when he hasn't had sleep."

The doctor looks at me and then back at Skye. "At the risk of taking my life into my own hands, you can actually return to work Monday. I want you to rest this weekend and do absolutely nothing, but as long as your ribs aren't giving you pain, and you feel up to it, you can resume normal duties Monday.

"Yay!" Skye says and I just bite my tongue.

"As long as those duties don't include pretending you're Mario Andretti," the doctor adds.

Skye laughs and they talk a few more minutes, while I quietly stew by the window. I look out, not really seeing anything. I'm mad. Skye doesn't take this threat seriously and she needs to. I'm going to have to work double time to keep her safe, because for some reason the woman refuses to see danger.

"Bull?" Skye asks, and it's only then that I notice the doctor has left.

"I don't want you to go back to work, Doc. Someone out there is trying to hurt you."

"You don't know that for sure."

"I do, every brake line on your car had been fucked with."

She takes that information in and her complexion goes white.

"Then you can have one of your men follow me around."

"Doc..." I start, because that's not good enough, at least not for me.

"He can follow me around, Bull. I won't even argue. The one thing I'm not going to do, is give up my life.

"Someone has a special delivery," that chick Judy comes in carrying a vase of red roses, two dozen to be exact. She been in more than anyone to check on Skye.

"Judy! You shouldn't have!" Skye says, reaching for the vase.

"Don't look at me girl, I can't afford this shit on my budget, especially after the house."

"Bull?"

"Wasn't me Doc, but I can tell you right now, if they're from that fucking Walter, I'm going to march them in his office and make him eat them."

Judy starts laughing. She probably thinks I'm kidding. *I'm not.*

"Bull. I doubt Walter would buy me flowers, especially after his last run-in with you."

"For his sake, Doc, I hope you're right."

She takes the card and reads it, and then her eyes find mine. Fear deep and thick stares back at me, and I know before I read the damned thing who they are from.

"Bull…"

Goddamn I'm starting to hate that tone coming from my woman. I reach for the card and the flowers.

The strongest ties are forged in fire. Do not make me hurt you again. We'll be together soon—AW.

I throw the flowers, vase, and all in the trash. Grab my phone and call Freak. The motherfucker ordered flowers. This time there has to be some kind of paper trail—*something.* He doesn't know who the fuck he's dealing with. But he will. I'll make sure he knows, right before I end him.

AW

HE'S STAYING BY her side like a guard dog. He is foolish enough to think she belongs to him. Skye has further punishment coming. She has let the sins of the flesh seduce her. I must cleanse her. I was hoping she would have learned her lesson, but as I stand outside her hospital room, watching her kiss another man, it is clear she has not.

I cannot stop the tears that fall from my eyes. She was so clean once. Now I will have to chase the blackness out of her soul. I hope she survives the fire.

My hand shakes as I continue down the hall. Why must they all choose the hard path? I had such hopes for Skye. I thought she was different.

I wanted her to be different.

Chapter 33

SKYE

"**D**R. WALKER, IF I might have a word," I look up at Dr. Eldridge and I want to scream. I don't have time for this idiot. It's Thanksgiving and I had to work. Holidays for a doctor, kind of suck—especially when you're the low man on the totem pole. Plus, I took Monday and Tuesday off so Bull would calm down. That meant when Walter fixed the rotation, he put me on duty yesterday and today—most likely because he's a douchebag. Still, I put in my time, and if I hurry home I will still get to have leftovers. Bull and Matty are already at Blair and David's. They get to have dinner with them and while that lessens the guilt of not being able to cook dinner for my family, it doesn't make me feel any better for not being there.

Family. I know there's a goofy smile on my face as I let that word repeat in my mind. *Matty and Bull are my family.* For so long it's just been me and Matty. Now, everything feels different. One look at Doctor Asshole, and the goofy smile is gone.

"Is there a problem, Dr. Eldridge?" I ask, trying to keep the hate out of my voice. I don't think I succeed.

"Cut the sarcasm, Dr. Walker."

I start to point out, I haven't used any yet, but it'd be pointless.

"Were you aware that you prescribed Mrs. Case in Room 402 the wrong antibiotic?"

"Excuse me?"

"You prescribed Bactrim for her infection. She's allergic to sulfa based drugs, if I hadn't caught it, the results could have been disastrous.

"There were no notations in her chart about a sulfa allergy. I checked and asked the patient myself if she had any allergies," I tell him reaching for the file.

He holds the file away from me, and then puts it under his arm, looking down at me.

"I read it myself. The notation is there, and Ms. Case is in her eighties. You know better than to rely on a patient's word. Especially, with her age and the symptoms she was presenting."

"I'm telling you when I had the file, there were no drug allergies listed."

That's when he whips out the file and opens it to the correct form. Sure enough, under known allergies, sulfa antibiotics is listed. The only problem is, that form was not there earlier today and that handwriting is definitely Dr. Eldridge's. I'm smelling a rat, but there's nothing I can do about it.

"I apologize Dr. Eldridge, I can only reiterate that, the allergy form was *not* in Ms. Case's file earlier today."

"So it just appeared out of the blue?"

"Or someone put it back in after the fact."

"Good Lord, Dr. Walker, at least own up to your mistake, don't go trying to lay the blame at another's feet. What possible reason could anyone have for doing something as heinous as that?"

"Make themselves look good? Ruin my career? I'm sure there are any number of reasons."

"Really, Dr. Walker. I'm afraid I have no recourse, but to report this to Dr. Reynolds."

Of course you don't. Normally it wouldn't bother me, but I already know I'm not on Walter's good list. There's little I can do here though. I turn to leave without saying another thing.

"Have you nothing to say for yourself Dr. Walker?"

"I have plenty to say, I just know it wouldn't help. Do whatever you want Dr. Eldridge, we both know you will anyway. Just be very careful, because believe me when I tell you, I will make it my life's mission to make sure you reap what you sew."

"Are you threatening me, Dr. Walker?"

"Whatever do you mean? I just said I wanted to make sure you got every *reward* you've worked for. Right? If I was threatening you, I would have said something about knowing the right combination of drugs to use so that your tiny pencil dick, that seems to be the talk in the nurse's lounge, never gets hard again. Now if you don't mind, I have a family to get home to." I leave with my parting remark. Dr. Eldridge is yelling, demanding to know what I'm talking about. I feel like my work here is done.

"Fucking bastard," I mumble, and then laugh.

If Bull heard me, I bet he'd reward me. I may have to let him know tonight after dinner. Lord knows, I'm going to need something to help me relax. Because, despite my bravado in front of that asshole, I know my meeting with Walter will not go well. Shit, maybe I should transfer out to another hospital? There's one in Corbin, I just hate the thought of the extra hour commute it will add to my day. My time with Matty is already limited. With a weary sigh, I exit the hospital. Time to be like Scarlet again, I decide. I'm just going to think about it tomorrow.

Chapter 34

BULL

"**W**HY ARE YOU carrying mom?" Matty asks, as we go through Skye's front door.

"She's worn out and full of turkey," I joke laying Skye down on the couch. I use her favorite afghan to cover her, then go back to make sure I locked the door. "Hey little dude, can you stay here with your mom while I check the house out?"

"Sure, whatever," Matty says, I get the feeling something is bothering him. I'll have to try and figure that out a little later.

Right now, I need to make sure the house is clear. I've had prospects watching the place all day, but you can't be too careful. It's a one story house, so it's relatively easy. I save Skye's room for last. It all seems fine, and the tension in my body eases slightly.

"All's good buddy," I tell Matty, when I come back in. He doesn't answer me for a minute, then nods. Without saying another word, he walks towards the hall. I have zero experience with children. But I do know that something has Matty upset. We've had a really good relationship, and I don't want anything to get in the way of that. "Do, you want to tell me what's wrong?" I finally ask.

Matty freezes, and turns to look at me. He studies me for a

minute, before letting me have it.

"Nick says you're only being nice to me because you're trying to get in my mom's pants."

Fuck. I wasn't expecting that. The kid's what nine? Hell, I know I grew up hard, but do kids with good homes really talk about this shit? This early?

"What did you tell him?"

"I punched him."

I laugh, walking over to Matty. I kneel down in front of him, putting my hand on his shoulder.

"Your mom would want me to tell you that fighting is not the way to handle things."

"Yeah, I know."

"As a man, I'm going to tell you what I really feel."

He looks worried, I don't want that. But, I need him to hear what I have to say.

"Men respect a good woman. They respect their family and they fight for them. They don't let anyone talk bad about them, so you were right to do what you did." He looks shocked, but then nods his head in agreement.

"So, are you just trying to get in my mom's pants?"

Jesus Christ.

"Matthew man to man here, I love your mom. I plan on being around a long time."

"How long?" he asks, his face giving nothing away.

"I want to marry her. I plan on raising a family with her."

His face looks hurt for a minute, and I know I've handled this wrong. *Hell.*

"You probably don't want me around then. You know, because I'm not your kid and all."

I put both hands on him and look him dead in the eye. I may not know kids, but I do know what it feels like to think you don't belong anywhere. That was me, before my stint in the service and then becoming a Savage member.

"Matthew. I love your mom. *Everything* about her. You're part of her and that automatically includes you."

"It does?" he asks, and I can hear the hope in his voice.

"It does, but I can tell you this Matthew. Even if I didn't know your mom, I'd still be proud to have you as a son."

His eyes grow large. "You mean that, Bull?"

"I absolutely mean that, Matthew. When I say I want a family with your mom that family wouldn't be anything without you too. You and your mom are my family. You understand what I'm saying?"

"I love you, Bull."

There are times when words grab a hold of your heart and squeeze the fuck out of it. It can be goodbyes, like it was when I lost my friend to cancer. It can be heartbreak, like I thought I had with Carrie. And then there are moments like this. When a kid that barely comes up to your hip, says four little words that completely unman you. Warmth flows through me, and for the life of me I can't think of a damn thing to say, so I just wrap my arms around the kid, and hold him tight.

"I love you too, buddy."

He pulls away, and that look he's been wearing on his face is gone now, replaced by a big smile. "So, you're going to be my dad now?"

"If I can talk your mom into it, absolutely."

"Good enough," he nods.

"Good enough," I tell him, my throat constricted with emotion. He runs off to his room, just before he gets to the door, I stop him. "Hey Matthew?"

"Yeah, Bull?"

"If you ever worry about picking a fight with someone?

Afraid you might not win? You wait until your family is there to back you up."

"My family?"

"Yeah. A man knows never to do things alone. Family, true family will always have your back. You're never alone. You hear me?"

"I hear you. I'm going to go play my game. If you want to kiss mom and stuff, so maybe she'll want you as my dad, I guess that's okay."

I try my best not to laugh. "I'll try that very thing."

"You might try picking her some of those white daisies out in the yard, or draw her pictures of horses. She really likes those. You need to give girls gifts if you want them to like you, Bull. Adam, from school told me that."

"He did?"

"Yeah, he gave Suzie one of his Wii games, and she let him kiss her."

"Is that a fact?"

"Yeah, but that won't work for you. Mom don't play video games. So, if I was you, I'd try the flowers and pictures."

"Thanks for the advice."

"Hey family has to have each other's backs."

"That's right," I say, and when he disappears into his room. I just remain sitting there. That kid rocked my world off its axis, and he has no idea.

"He's right you know."

I straighten up at the sound of Skye's voice, and look over my shoulder at her. She still looks half asleep, but the tears on her cheeks and the smile on her face tell me that she's been awake long enough to hear my exchange with Matthew.

"About what, Doc?" I ask, wondering how I got to be such a lucky son of a bitch.

"If you give me a present, I might let you kiss me."

"Is that a fact?"

"Oh, yeah."

"I don't have any daisies, and God's honest truth, I can't draw worth a damn."

"Well that is a problem," she says. I stand up, turn, and wait for her.

"It is, because I sure could use a kiss."

"Maybe you have something you could give me instead," she whispers, walking into my arms.

"What would that be?"

"I don't know. Maybe we could talk about it and something will come to me."

"You don't say?"

"Yeah, I'm sure if we talk long enough, something will *pop up* that will interest me," she says, her hand sliding under my shirt."

"I think that sounds like a great plan."

"I was hoping you'd feel that way."

"How long is it before Matthew will go to sleep, Doc?" I whisper against her lips.

"A couple of hours," she says, and I stop her hand from reaching my chest.

"Oh God, I'm going to be in hell."

"I'll make it worth it, Bull. *I'll make it worth it*," she says with a smile, before my mouth claims hers.

Chapter 35

BULL

"IS HE DOWN?" I ask Skye, lying on the bed in some gym shorts. Waiting...for her.

"Out like a light. You're looking awful comfortable."

"I was just lying here thinking," I tell her, putting my arms behind my head as a pillow, my eyes never leaving hers.

"I'm almost afraid to ask," she jokes. "Exactly what were you thinking?"

"You have the prettiest tits I've ever seen."

She laughs, "You are definitely a boob man."

"*Definitely.* But you know what Doc? I don't think I've got to see your tits bounce when you're riding me."

"Have I mentioned how romantic you are?"

"Maybe once or twice. Don't much feel like being romantic right now, though."

"Why's that?"

"I want you naked and straddling me."

"Bull..."

"I want you to wrap your hand around my cock and guide me inside that tight, little cunt of yours."

"God..."

"Then I want you to use my dick like your own personal playground. I just want to lie here and watch you as you use me to make yourself come."

She unties the belt of her robe, and slips out of it. It falls, revealing her gorgeous body, and landing at her feet. My dick was already hard, but now the fucker is standing straight up, begging for attention.

"Take your shorts off, Bull," she tells me, her voice hoarse, like she always gets when she's wet and needy.

"I think you forgot how fucking me works, Skye. Maybe I need to spank your ass to remind you," I tell her, and I can physically see the way the excitement flares in her body.

"I..."

"You what?"

"Will you please, take your clothes off, Bull?"

Fuck. *She destroys me.* I reach down and yank my shorts off, kicking them out of the way. My cock stands tall, demanding attention. Pre-cum has already coated the head and a pearl white strand slides down the side. I grab my dick at the base, squeezing tight. My damn balls are right there, already full, wanting to release in her. I look at Skye and catch her licking her lips.

"See something you like, Doc?"

"God, yes," she breathes, and her hand moves down to her pussy, its lips already coated in her arousal.

"Skye, if those fingers touch anywhere near your clit, you don't get to come tonight."

Her hand freezes—just like I knew it would.

"Now, I want you to straddle me at my knees." She looks confused at my command, but does it. Her sweet little cunt is a few inches from my cock. Too far to fuck, but definitely close enough to tease. "Use your hands to hold your pussy open for me, Skye."

I love the way her soft pale skin flushes with a mixture of

embarrassment and heat. She's fucking perfection.

"Like this?" she asks self-consciously. She's using her fingers to pull her lips apart, and her sweet cunt is displayed like the prize it is. It's covered with her need, so shiny and slick, I could come for days using nothing more than this memory.

"Exactly like that. Doc, your clit is throbbing."

"I know," she whimpers.

"Do you need something, sweetheart?"

"Yes…" she hisses.

"What do you need?"

"Bull…"

I slap my cock against her hard clit. She leans towards me and I reward her by rubbing the hard head of my dick up and down her pussy. I can feel her body tremble, and nearly moan as her pussy tries to suck my cock inside, when I push it against her hot, creamy. *Made for me.* Fucking hell, this woman was made for me.

"Sweet, Jesus," she gasps.

I slap my cock against her again, two more times and it's such a good fucking feeling, this time tremors run through *my* body. I rub the head of my cock against her clit, dragging it down almost to her entrance. The tip breaches her this time and she freezes. Her eyes look down at me, hazy and dilated.

"Bull…what about…I mean…protection?"

I slide back up her pussy until I reach her clit, and rub against it in small half-circles. She starts grinding against me. Her body softly thrusting, her back is arched, and her breasts are pushed out. *Beautiful.*

"Are you on the pill?"

"Yes…" she whimpers.

"Then I'm fucking you bare. I'm clean. You've seen the records. I don't want anything between us, Skye."

Her eyes look into mine and she nods in agreement, but that's not good enough.

"The words, Skye. Give me the words."

"Yes, I want you bare inside of me. I want to feel…"

"Feel what baby?"

"Feel your cock…." she gasps, because I'm rubbing the tip of my cock harder and harder against her clit. "What are you doing to me?" she cries, her body trying to rotate the same direction my cock does—just to prolong the sensations.

"I'm fucking your clit. Do you like it baby?" I ask her, as I outline her opening with my finger. Her sweetness is thick, and I gather it up, and then bring my finger to my mouth, sucking it clean. *Mine.* Skye is watching me. White teeth bite into her plump lips. There's no way she could know how fucking sexy she is.

"Yes. Bull, please. Make me come."

What man could resist the woman of his dreams, asking that? I thrust a finger into her while still using my cock to tease her clit. Her pussy closes around my finger, the soft skin flutters around it, as her walls tremble. I slide another finger in and fuck her with both. All I have to do is hold my cock against her clit, because her greedy little body is doing all the work now. She's rubbing off on my cock, while I thrust my fingers in and out of her.

"Fuck. Oh God. Fuck me, Bull," she whimpers.

My balls draw up wanting to join her. It turns me on like nothing else, when I get those prim and proper lips of hers, to cry out fuck.

"I got you baby. I'm fucking this juicy little cunt. Are you going to come for me, Skye?"

Her body quakes, rocking back and forth. I can't stop from groaning out loud as I watch her cum slide out of her pussy and caress my hand.

"I'm coming!" she cries out, sliding against my cock so hard and fast it's amazing to watch.

When the final quake moves through her body, my hands bite into her ass and I pull her over my cock.

"Hold my dick, Skye, hold it so I can get inside you. *Now*," I growl, because growling is all I'm capable of at the moment.

She does as I ask. Then, using the hold I have on her ass, I shove her down on my dick hard. She cries out. She wants to move—I don't let her. I hold her still. I close my eyes, because they nearly roll back in my head at the feelings bombarding me. The inner muscles of her pussy clamp down on my cock. She's doing her best to pull away from my hold, wanting to ride me. Again, I don't let her. I need this. I want to memorize every fucking thing about this. This is probably as close as I will ever get to a religious experience. She's my fucking altar, and I plan on worshipping her the rest of my life.

"Bull! Fuck me!"

I grin, reach up, and pinch her nipple. She probably thinks it's to punish her, but it's definitely to reward her.

"I told you, Doc. I'm just going to lay here. You get to fuck yourself on my cock."

She looks at me, and then she surprises the fuck out of me. Because she smiles. It's a smile that could make men grown men quake in their shoes. She rises up on my cock and slams back down. Once I'm balls deep, she rotates her hips, and grinds her pussy against my body.

I can do nothing but watch as she rides me, and all too soon I'm screaming out in release. I empty every last fucking drop of cum I have inside of her.

Chapter 36

BULL

"**H**EY MAN! HOW in the hell did you manage to get uglier while we were gone?" Dancer says, and I throw him the middle finger.

"Fuck you," I joke, slapping him on the back. Dragon comes in, carrying Nicole and I just shake my head. He's always carting her around. I think if it was up to him, she'd never walk. "Jesus did you knock her up again?"

Dragon stops and smirks at me. Nicole is sound asleep in his arms. Behind him, Gunner who picked them up at the airport, comes in holding Little D—Dragon and Nicole's baby boy. He holds the door open for Carrie, and she comes in holding her and Dancer's little girl. She's a cute little thing with her mommy's red hair.

At one time the sight of Carrie holding the baby might have hurt me. Now, all I can think about is Skye, and what it would feel like if she was holding my baby—*our baby*.

"Hey man, everything going okay?" Dragon asks.

"Yeah, it's been quiet since the hospital man," I tell him reaching for Jazz.

Faith Jasmine Blake is a beautiful little baby who looks just like her mom, and very little like her dad. Well maybe his eyes, but she's her mom made over. We all call her Jazz, since the name is after the sister that Dancer lost. Dancer also named her faith, because he said it was Carrie's faith in him that helped him to survive.

"There's my girl. Come give your Uncle Bull some love. What a pretty girl you are. Thank God you look nothing like your daddy."

"I can't say anything but amen to that," Dance agrees. "She's her mom made over."

"She has your eyes Jacob," Carrie interjects, walking to me and putting a pacifier in Jazz's mouth. "Hey, Dorian, you're looking better," she says, leaning up, and kissing me on the cheek.

If I was still hung up on her, that would have killed me. I'm pretty sure it could make Dancer kill me *now*. Carrie is too naïve to know what it would have done to me, and she laughs off the way Dance gets jealous. She's young, she has a lot to learn. Skye isn't much older, but she's been seasoned by life. I'm starting to realize just how well she fits me. I also hate when Carrie says my name. *Despise it.* I could kill Dancer for letting her know my real name. Skye instinctively settled into calling me Bull. We just click. *Fucking hell, do we click!*

"I'm good, Carrie. I'd be even better if you guys would just give it up, and give me little Jazz here."

"Not on your fucking life."

"Jacob! Don't use that language around the babies!" Carrie admonishes.

"Yeah, stop it," Nicole mumbles. Dragon sets down and Nicole curls in his lap. She's awake now, but she's got her head on Dragon's chest, and she looks like she's about to go back out at any second.

"Hey little Mama," I tell her, ignoring Dragon's scowl.

"Hey, Bull. Did you have a good Thanksgiving? I wish you

had come with us," Nicole says.

"Damn it Nicole, I have to have some men here watching shit," Dragon grumbles, but I grin.

Even if there wasn't a reason for it, he'd rather I be far away from Nicole. She and I got pretty close when he pretended to be dead. We are just friends, but any reminder of that time pisses Drag off. It's fun sometimes to fuck with him about it. Truth is, I wouldn't have left either way. I would never think of leaving Skye. I would like to take her and Matty to see Crush and Dani someday though.

"Dragon! Stop with the language! Dom's first words will get him kicked out of preschool!"

"Damn it woman, he can barely gurgle. I doubt he's going to wake up and say, *'Fuck you, mommy,'* any time soon."

"If you don't stop using those words, you will wake up someday soon, and *you* won't get to *fuck mommy* for a very long time," she warns him.

"You wouldn't dare," he growls.

"Try me," she replies, sounding deadly serious.

"I'm going to smack that ass when we're alone."

"Always with the promises," she sighs, snuggling back down in his lap.

Dragon kisses the top of her head.

"This crew is crazier than heck fire, little Jazz," I coo at the baby.

"Heck fire?" Gunner speaks up, still holding Dom. "I swear my balls are going to shrivel up if I hang around here much more."

I laugh. "One of Skye's words. It must be a mom thing, she doesn't like to use bad words around Matthew either."

"Oh, how is the, pretty Doctor?" Gunner says.

"Fuck you. You best stay away from Skye!" I growl.

"Bull!" Carrie and Nicole say at the same time.

Dancer and Dragon laugh, and finally I join in, after I shoot Gunner a look that I hope *does* make his balls shrivel up.

"Any more threats against your woman?" Drag asks when it dies down.

"Nah man, it's been quiet. Skye has been a little more cautious since the thing with her brakes, but nothing else has really happened. She wants to believe it's over now."

"But you don't think so?" Dancer asks, pulling Carrie into him and looping his hands around her waist.

"My gut tells me it's more."

"Is there anything in her life that could come back to bite us all in the ass?" Dragon asks, and I know he's thinking about Dani, and all of the hell we went through. Nicole must know the same because she kisses him on his neck, hugging him tighter.

"Nah, Skye doesn't have contact with her family anymore. They cut her off when she got pregnant with Matthew."

"What fuckwads," Nicole says and everyone turns to look at her. "*What?* Some people require cursing," she huffs.

She's not wrong.

"What about the kid's dad?" Dragon continues.

"He's never been in the picture. Never wanted anything to do with Matthew, even signed over all rights to him."

"Damn," Nicole murmurs. I agree, but I'm glad it turned out this way, because I'm more than happy to be the man, his ass wouldn't be.

"She's been having trouble at work," I tell them. "I handled one asshole, but she's got a meeting today about some shit with another doctor."

"What about that nurse?" Carrie pipes up.

"She's still MIA. No one has seen her since I kicked her

out of the club the other night."

"That doesn't seem like the Melissa I know," Dragon says.

"Just how well do you know her?" Nicole huffs.

"Calm your ass woman. I'm innocent here. Bull's the one who spent time sticking it to her."

"Don't remind me," Skye says, coming towards me.

I didn't see her come in. I am fucking glad to see her, but I kind of wish she had picked a different moment to walk in. I'd rather she had missed this portion of the conversation. I don't want to remind her of what an idiot I was. I decide it's okay, because she walks straight to me. I open my arms, and she steps into them, wrapping her arms around me, and holding me close. I return the favor, breathing in her sweet scent. A man could get used to this. I kicked one addiction, but I can admit that I am addicted to this woman. I'm pretty sure, she's an addiction I'll never be able to quit.

"Hey, Doc," I tell her, and her lips softly. Not the kiss I want to give her, but I can't resist a small taste.

"Mmmm…" she says, as our lips break apart. Then, she buries her head into my chest.

"That bad, baby?" I ask, worried about her, because I can feel the stress rolling off of her.

She lets out a large, frustrated growl.

"Walter put me on administrative leave, pending an internal investigation."

"That fu……..."

Skye's hand clamps over my mouth. "Bull! There are babies in here!"

"Jesus Christ!" I'm going to go out and shoot shit or something. *Hell, anything!* It's too fucking girly in here. I need something to make hair grow on my balls," Gunner grumbles, handing baby Dom over to Dancer.

Skye pulls away to look at Gunner while everyone starts laughing. She's been to the club a few times now, and she likes to give Gunner a hard time.

"Women don't like hairy balls," she informs him.

"They'll like them, and they will suck them when they get a look at what comes with them," Gunner winks, before he leaves the room.

"Goddamn it! Stop talking about sucking balls around Jazz," Dancer yells.

"What's wrong, Daddy? Worried some fucker is going to get in her pants, like you did her mama's?" Dragon jokes.

"Fuck you," Dancer growls, in spite of Carrie giving him the stink-eye.

"You should have had a boy like me," Dragon says.

"Funny, I don't remember you going through labor," Nicole says quietly.

Dragon must decide to ignore her. "With Dom, all I have to do is sit back, throw condoms at him, and pat him on the back."

"The hell you do! No son of mine is going to be the horn dog that you were, Dragon," Nicole argues.

"I didn't hear you complaining, Mama."

"Then you didn't see me punching one of your freaking Twinkies. *Our* son will save himself for someone special."

"Fuck you're trying to turn him into a pussy," Dragon says, and he sounds sick already.

"Whatever. You two just make sure you keep your boy away from Jazz," Dancer says.

"*Oh! Carrie!* Can you imagine if Dom and Jazz fell in love?" Nicole asks, sounding way too excited.

"*Oh, wow!*" Carrie cries.

"*That'd be amazing!*" the girls say together.

"That'd be a fucking disaster!" the men say at the same time.

"Fuckin' A, now I need a drink," Dragon grumbles, standing up and letting Nicole slide to her feet. He kisses her gently, letting his thumb brush against the side of her face. She smiles at him, and just like always, it seems as if the world fades away for those two.

"C'mon boys, let's have church," Dragon orders, heading off to his office. Dancer hands little Dom to Nicole to follow after Dragon.

"Carrie?" Skye whispers. She has a strange look on her face, and I got a feeling this is not going to be a good conversation.

"We'll talk later, Doc. You get to know Nic and Carrie, and I'll be back."

I see how she wants to argue, but she doesn't. I promise myself that I'll make it up to her later.

Chapter 37

BULL

"**S**O? THE DOCTOR?" Dragon says, once we get settled, and he has one of the Twinkies bring us some drinks.

It's just the three of us. Freak, Hawk, and Gunner are all missing. Six and Nailer just come in during special meetings. Dragon's been extra cautious after all of the shit over the last couple of years. I guess this is to be an informal meeting. It doesn't matter, I'd lay claim Skye in front of all of them.

"She's mine."

"Another one bites the dust," Dancer says motioning his beer to me.

"Damn straight," I agree, because I've never been happier in my fucking life.

"Jesus, we got old and boring."

"Shut your mouth. There's not a fucking thing boring about me," Dragon says, shooting Dancer the finger. "Now let's get serious. I didn't want to talk about this in front of the girls, but be honest, how worried should we be about the threat on Skye?"

"My fucking skin is crawling. It's been quiet since her accident, but something is coming and it's killing me that I can't stop it."

"Did Freak find anything from the flower order?"

"Fucker called the order in from a burner cell. He used a prepaid Visa card for the payment."

"Let me guess, there's no way to trace the fucking burner," Dance says.

"Nothing so far. Freak traced the prepaid card purchase to a dollar store outside of London."

"Security cameras?" Dragon asks.

"Freak's pouring through them, but we don't know who we're looking for, so it's like a fucking needle in a haystack," I tell him, disgusted. I hate not being able to get ahead of this motherfucker.

"The police?"

"Treating it like a fucking joke, man. Probably because she's mine."

"That sounds about right," Dragon says, tiredly. "Do you think the threat has to do with the club, or her in general? Maybe her work?"

"I want to say work, I don't see what else it could be. Skye goes out of her way to help others, Drag. Shit, there's folks knocking down her door just to help her. She's good people."

"I can tell that by the way she's brought you back," Dragon says, watching me closely.

"I lost my way. I'm finding it again."

"You need to see the shrink that Nicole and Carrie set me up with. She's cool as hell. It might sound hokey, but it helps brother," Dancer says.

"I'll think about it. But I've been sober for a while now and to be honest I don't really have an urge to go back where I was. If I could get rid of these fucking headaches and tremors…" I growl.

"They haven't got any better?" Dragon asks, concerned. He should be, as the club enforcer I have a lot of the club's business on my shoulders. Right now, I'm not sure I could do the job. Luckily, the club seems to have evened out after the mess with Dani and her ex.

"Nah, man. Not really. Skye's been using pressure points to dull my headaches and that's helped. Damn quacks at the hospital want to say it's a triggered response—psychosomatic bullshit, or something like that. There's no way this fucking shit is in my head. It feels like knives stabbing my eyes out sometimes, and you've seen the tremors."

'I know you don't want to hear it man, but I'm telling you I think Trisha could help with that," Dancer says.

"Trisha?"

"The shrink. She's good. At least I think so. She and Gunner seem to bump heads. He came with me to pick up some papers, and they were like oil and water. They know each other. Gunner and her brother are tight or something."

I hold my head down. I really don't want to agree to see a shrink. Skye has been on me about it though. Hell, I don't know, maybe it would help.

"I'll think about it," I finally agree. I don't think it will help, but I'm willing to try about anything to be normal again. My biggest worry is that something will happen, and I won't be able to protect Skye.

"Okay back to the problem at hand. I'll have Freak look into the doctors giving Skye flack. I'll get him to check into that damned nurse too. Something about her just disappearing doesn't sit right with me. But, she could have struck out at Skye before disappearing. If she attacked one of her own? Well, she's been a hanger on long enough to know how dangerous that is. It'd make sense she ran," Dragon tells us.

"You know what happens when a woman is scorned," Nicole pipes up.

"Woman what have I told you about coming in here?" Dragon asks her, but he doesn't look upset. Then again, he didn't close the door either, so I doubt he cares.

"To bend over the table?" she answers.

Dragon shakes his head, but he smiles. Hell, he always smiles these days.

"I need the keys to the Suburban, we left Dom's diaper bag in it," she tells him.

He reaches down into his pocket and pulls them out. She reaches for them, but he pulls them back.

"Where's my kiss woman?

"Always on my ass," she mumbles.

"Just wait till later," Dragon tells her, and damn if she doesn't blush.

"Sounds like Nicole thinks it might be Melissa," Dancer says, once she leaves.

"She's a smart woman," Dragon says, staring off into space, and you can tell he's thinking everything over. He puts his beer back down and stares at it. "My woman is smart as they come. I got a look at what happens if a woman feels like she's been wronged, it can get ugly. And when the woman is as fucked up as that bitch, Melissa? I'd say it'd pay to keep an eye on her.

"If we can find her," Dance adds.

"Fucking hell, women complicate everything," Dragon mumbles.

"Maybe Nicole was right about waiting for one woman to fuck," Dancer says.

It doesn't escape my notice that not a damned one of us argues. Instead we all remain quiet and drink our beer.

Chapter 38

BULL

I RAKE MY hand over my head. I just got Matthew down for the night, and Skye is passed out on the couch asleep. She's had a rough day, she's back at work, but she's miserable, and she's talking about switching hospitals. The nearest one would add an hour driving time to her day. That doesn't thrill me. I've been toying with the idea of using my connections to have her problems dealt with. It wouldn't make Skye happy, but it sure would me.

I decide to keep busy while my family is resting. Despite the stress of the day, I love that I have a family now. I will move heaven and earth to keep them safe. I pull Skye's ugly old afghan over her, and then go into the bathroom. I'm way too keyed up to rest. I keep my head bare, but I've let it slide the last few days. I can feel the stubble and hate it.

I hunt up the things I'll need and line them up on the bathroom sink. I heat a wash towel with hot water, and place it over my head. Once that's done, and I've let it rest long enough, I get out my razor and shaving cream.

"You use a disposable razor?" I look in the mirror, and Skye's leaning against the doorway watching me. She's wearing one of my thermal shirts, and nothing else. Her hair is mussed, she looks sleepy and tired. She's never looked more beautiful to me.

"Electric ones leave razor burn."

"Sit down and I'll do it for you."

"I don't know that I've ever trusted a woman to shave my head."

"Then I definitely want it, there should be one part of you I'll be the first to get," she says, already reaching for the razor.

"There is, Doc. My heart."

Her eyes go soft. "Give me that razor. I don't need to cry because my man is good with lines."

I hand her the razor with a grin. "I'm not sure this is going to work. I'm a little tall for you."

She closes the lid on the toilet and stands by it before bowing and laughing. "Your throne awaits, kind sir."

"My throne? Am I king of the porcelain now?" I ask her sitting down.

"King of my heart," She says starting to shave me.

"Now who's good with lines?" I ask her. She laughs, but doesn't say anything else.

"What are you thinking, Doc?" I ask, when she finishes and is rinsing out the razor and cleaning up.

She stops and looks at me through the bathroom mirror with a sad smile. "I was thinking I'm very grateful for you, Bull."

"It's going to be okay, Doc." I tell her, praying I'm right.

"I know," she says, putting on the lotion I always use after shaving. "Do you know what I didn't know?" she asks.

I enjoy the feel of her hands on me. This is what I want for the rest of my life. *This is my future.*

"What's that?"

"That Carrie is alive. You said you lost her."

Her words shock me. I hadn't got a chance to talk with her

about Carrie. I admit it was mostly because I didn't want to. I knew I would eventually. What I wasn't expecting was that she was upset, because she thought Carrie was dead.

"I meant I lost her to Dancer. Carrie's been in love with him since she was a little girl."

"Well obviously I know that *now*, Bull. How did you ever fall in love with a woman that your friend claimed?"

"They weren't together. Hell, I wouldn't do that, Skye. Dancer killed a man who attacked Carrie. He got sent up and the club took her in when someone threatened her life. I cared about her. Hell, Skye's she's a sweet person."

She sighs, and puts the lotion up, walks over to the sink, and puts away my things.

"Skye? Talk to me."

"She is sweet."

"Yeah," I agree, wondering if I should.

"I can't help but notice that she looks a lot like me," she says, and there's a hint of accusation in her voice. Her eyes level on me through the mirror of the medicine cabinet.

"She does not," I deny, and I can feel anger building inside of me. I don't know what I expected, but this wasn't it.

Skye turns on me, and crosses her arms. "Come on, Bull. *The hair?* Hell even our bodies are built similarly. If you wanted a substitute..."

"Don't say it, Skye," I caution her.

"What? That I'm just..."

"Doc, I'm warning you not to go there."

"Why not? It's like a giant elephant in the room!"

"Only in your own mind! Fucking hell woman, do you not see me? Is everything I'm doing just not getting through to you? I love *you*. I haven't said that to another fucking woman."

"Not even..."

"Only fucking you, Skye."

"Oh. I thought…"

"I know what you thought."

"Bull…"

"Is this what our lives are going to be like? You spend time making up reasons to push me away?"

"I am not."

"Yes, you are. I've jumped through hoops for you, and yet every damn time I turn around you're coming up with something else to throw in my face, or to not tell me how you feel."

"Bull…"

"I'm a fucking grown ass man. A man who is the club enforcer for one of the baddest fucking clubs around, and yet you've got me wrapped around your finger like a damned…"

"I do not! And if you are so miserable…"

"I'm not miserable! I'm right where I want to be, but I'm tired of you doubting me! Treat me like a motherfucking man!"

"I know you're a man!"

"No, you don't. You think I'm a grown boy, who doesn't know his own mind! You think I can't wipe my own ass!"

"That's so not true!"

"You think I'm fucked up enough that I would try and make you a replacement for another woman!"

"Well…"

"And before that, you thought I was using you as a reason to stay sober."

"Bull…"

And before that, I was just looking to get my dick wet, right?"

"You're twisting things…"

"That's easy to do when you tell a woman you love her,

and she has trouble meeting your eyes."

"Bull…"

"If you weren't ever going to forgive me for how we met, Skye. You should have just told me."

"I…Bull, that's not it! I do forgive you! I just…"

"You just don't trust me. Hell maybe you never will," I tell her walking out.

"Where are you going?"

"To the club. I need a drink."

"Are you coming back home?"

I don't answer. I just slam the door behind me. Let her worry.

AW

I WATCH AS he leaves—mad and angry. Joy spreads through me. I've been forced into watching Skye from a distance. Having him leave like this, gives me hope. I look through my binoculars and see her standing at the door crying. Crying over someone so far beneath her.

My joy is replaced by anger.

It's time I stop stalling.

It's time she learned.

I will teach her. I will train her. She will learn…in time…or else…

She wasn't truly the one.

Chapter 39

BULL

"I 'LL HAVE ONE of whatever he's having."

I look up from my drink to see Dragon sit down beside me. He picks up my Tom Collins and swirls it around in the glass.

"Fucking hell, has that doctor turned you into a pansy ass? Cancel that, Six. Get me a Jack on the rocks."

"Kiss my ass," I grumble, taking another drink.

"Looks too much like your face," he comes back. I flip him off. "What's up with you anyways?"

"Woman troubles."

"Amen," Dragon says, and takes a drink, before slamming it back on the table.

"Trouble in paradise?" I ask him, because fuck he has it made with Nic. We all know it.

"Fucking women man. Life is so much simpler without them."

"Truth," I tell him taking a drink.

"Nowhere near as fucking good though," Dragon says, staring off into space.

I grunt, it's all I have in me.

"She wants another baby. *She wants another fucking baby.*"

"So give her one."

"Fuck man, I almost lost her and Dom the last time. I don't think the universe wants me to have kids," Dragon grumbles, finishing his drink. He signals Six to bring him another one.

"Quit bitching. Your woman accepts you like you are, and still fucking wants you. Give her a baby."

"The Doc, giving you problems?"

"She doesn't trust me. She questions everything I tell her. *Hell.* I don't know if she will ever believe me. It wouldn't surprise me if she thought me being a club member is just a way to relive my childhood."

"Fuck."

"That's about the size of it, Drag."

"Remember when the biggest problem we had was how to shut a motherfucker up?"

"Gun, bomb or good old fashioned torture," I tell him, leaning back in my chair.

"Those were the fucking days," Dragon says.

"You going to knock your old lady up?"

"Well I sure ain't going without sex, so probably," he growls finishing his drink. "You going to show the Doc what being a member of the crew is all about?"

"Fuck, I don't know man."

"I take it telling her about Dancer's Christmas present would probably freak her the fuck out."

"Tell her we got four men chained up in the shed waiting for Dancer to blow their fucking heads off or whatever else he wants to do to them? Yeah, I'm thinking that'd send her running."

"So treat Skye, like Dance does Red," he says spinning his glass around.

"How's that?"

"Tell her nothing specific, but let her know you handle your shit."

"Hell man, I thought that's what I was doing. This woman has me all upside down. I feel like I'm spending every fucking day walking on eggshells."

"Why?" he asks and it's a damn good question.

"Fuck man from the moment we met, I've been a screw up. She knows I had the clap man. I feel like a fucking..."

"Stop talking about your feelings motherfucker. Do you make sure she can't walk after you give her dick?"

I laugh at his question, which comes out more like a snort. "Or talk," I tell him.

"Then she's got shit to complain about. I'd say your problem is, you're trying too damn hard."

"That's rich coming from the asshole who doesn't let his woman walk."

"Hell, that's not for her, I just like the way it feels to have her ass in my hands. Makes my dick hard," he says, before getting up, and slapping me on the back. "Go back to your woman. Leave no doubt in her mind that you're a fucking man, and not one she could replace. And instead of fixing her breakfast, eat her for breakfast. Treat her like you would a Twinkie."

"Skye's not a Twinkie, Drag man, she's special," I growl, because she is. "She's classy, smart, funny, and she doesn't need any fucker..."

"She's a woman. You can treat her special. But there ain't a woman around who doesn't want it hard and dirty. They appreciate a man who gives them that."

"But I do..."

"Even outside of bed. Fuck! Why in the hell do you think I spend so much time fucking my woman in the back room?"

"So the brothers can hear her scream?"

"Hell no. Though I got to admit, I enjoy the fuck out of that shit. I'd much rather be in a damn bed with her though. I do it because it makes her hotter than hell. She likes it dirty, and I like being the motherfucker lucky enough to give that to her."

"So you think sex can cure anything?"

"No, but it can damn sure make the rest easier to swallow," he says walking off.

"Where the fuck you going?" I ask him.

"Off to find Nicole," he calls back.

"And knock her up?"

"Probably, but she's going to fucking swallow a few times to earn that shit."

Chapter 40

BULL

ADDICTION IS A funny thing. Even when you don't want the shit, there's a part deep inside of you that craves it. I'm lying on the bed in my room at the Savage compound. After Dragon left, I didn't know what to do with my sorry ass. So, I came back here thinking I would sleep. That hasn't worked. All I keep thinking about is, Skye. Outside in the main room there's a party is in full swing. I didn't want to be there, but I shouldn't be here either.

I look at the bottle of pills I'm holding in my hand, staring at them, and even now, thinking how it'd be easier to live with them. My hand tightens on them, and the urge to down them is there. *It's screaming at me.*

Instead, I throw them across the room. Somewhere in the back of my mind I know that'd be a decision I couldn't rebound from. That'd be something that would forever put Skye out of my reach. The bottle crashes against the wall hard enough that the lid pops off, and pills scatter on the concrete floor.

I'm pissed and the kicker is that it's not even at Skye. I'm a fucking idiot. I've been trying to be perfect for her, instead of just being myself. No wonder she doesn't trust me. I haven't even tried showing her all of me. She probably does think I'm part of some kind of useless club. She hasn't even seen that side of me.

Hell, I should have just walked away from Skye, and never tried to reach for her. I knew she was out of my league. I rub the top of my head, I haven't taken a thing, I've not even had a drink, but my brain feels cloudy as hell. Is this what loving a woman does to your ass? No wonder my brothers always acted like fools. I sure as hell won't be giving Dragon flack now.

Even now, I have the urge to run back to Skye with my tail between my legs, but I don't. I just can't get past the fact...fuck I don't know what I can't get over—but I think it has a lot to do with the fact that Skye won't let her defenses down around me.

I leave the room feeling not one fucking bit better about shit. I just know I need to get out of there before the walls close in on me. I decide to get on my bike and ride, that always clears my head and maybe then I can go back to Skye and try and work this out.

"Hey man, where ya going?" I look over at Six, and he's sitting at the bar alone. He's all fucked up since he and Lips broke up. Lips went back home to Chicago, and Six didn't want to move with her. He's turned into a sorry sack of shit since she left. Hell, if he was going to grieve himself to death over her, he should have just followed her. Would I leave the state to follow Skye? I'm pretty fucking sure the answer would have been yes. That is, if she would just give herself to me completely. Fuck, if I'd kept her as long as Six had Lips? And Skye loved me the way Lips obviously did Six? *There wouldn't be a fucking question.*

"I'm going to go ride my bike for a bit man, clear my head," I tell him, going over and slapping him on his shoulder.

"Bullshit man. Come have a drink with me," he says, and

his words are starting slur, so I can tell he's been at it awhile.

I sit down reluctantly, I know what it means to lose a woman you care about. I might not have been in love with Carrie, but it still hurt.

"Beer," I tell one of the new prospects. I haven't even learned the kid's name. I heard Freak and Dragon call him numb nuts—I hope for his sake he doesn't end up with that road name.

I take a drink, before turning to face Six.

"Dude why don't you just give this shit up and go get your woman?"

"She left man. I ain't begging no pussy," he huffs.

"Lips is a good woman, Six. They ain't easily found," I tell him, but I can tell there's no talking sense into his ass.

"The fuck you say! There's good pussy everywhere!" he slurs back, and spins his barstool around to watch the girls dancing. "There's some good pussy right there. Come over here girls and give me and my brother some loving."

I hold my head down. When he yells over at the Twins. That's their names, they probably have individual ones, but I haven't taken the time to know them. They're good women, I'm not saying that. In fact, of all the women I've been with here in the club, I probably respect them the most. I worried that I might have passed some shit on to them after Skye gave me my diagnosis, but Melissa was the only one that had sucked my cock and I meant what I had told Skye, I keep my shit wrapped up when I'm fucking. I don't usually go from pussy to pussy either. I tend to find one and settle in until I get bored. I may have not wanted Melissa's pussy since the first time, but I wanted the pills she could give my sorry ass. Then, once I got the pills, I didn't give a fuck where I got off, or with whom. I just wanted to quit thinking. Goddamn! I'm a twisted fucker.

Skye would be better off without me.

I'm starting to feel the walls closing in on me. Now was usually the time I would reach for pills, but I'm not going down that road again. Time for me to go hop on my bike. Before I can make my move, one of the Twins glides into my lap, wraps her arm around the back of my neck, and pulls my face into her boobs. Before Skye, I would have definitely dived into them. *Before Skye I would have done a lot more.* Now that I've had Doc, I have no interest.

"Listen Six, buddy I'm going to head out. I got some shit to do," I tell him, pulling my head away.

"Aw, c'mon man. The Twins are in the mood to party."

"Sure are," the girls say, almost together.

The one in my lap starts sucking on the side of my neck. Jesus, how can something that feels so good, make my damn cock stand up and take notice, and yet, make my skin crawl?

I'm busy trying to pull away from her, to get the hell out of here, so I ignore the door when it opens. *Oh, but I hear her voice....*

"I'm looking for Bull? I'm his..."

"Skye?" I interrupt her, before I can stop my big mouth. The smart thing would be to fucking hide—or dump the girl on the floor. *Shit any of those!* No, I just sit there like an idiot with a semi-hard-on, staring at my woman in disbelief. I think my day just went from bad to fucking shit.

Chapter 41

SKYE

I NSANE. THAT'S WHAT I am. I don't know what I'm doing. After Bull left, I just kept getting more upset. I couldn't contain it. He's not completely right. I *do* think he's a man. He's an amazing man, and I love him. I have been keeping him at a distance, however. I'm terrified to drop my final defenses and let him in. I may have told him I loved him, but I did it when I thought I was dying, and besides, he never heard me. Knowing all of that, I haven't tried to tell him since.

I don't want to lose him because I'm afraid. It's time I move, and jump in with both feet, because I haven't. *I can do this.* I hold life in my hands at work every day! Surely I can handle a relationship with a biker who scares the hell out of me.

My bravado stays in place all the way there, until I get out of my car. There's definitely a party going on, I understand why Nicole warned me. Now, I'm almost ready to run back home. There's people out in the parking lot around a big bonfire. It's dark, but there's a street lamp, and I can see some man getting a blow job, there's women dancing naked...

Nicole warned me the parties here can get pretty wild. What will I see if I go inside? Do I really want to? I click the door locks on my keychain, the sound of my car's horn makes me jump. I give myself a pep talk all the way to the door. I stand there, unsure what to do. My courage has taken a nosedive. I jump when the door opens and a man comes out in a vest like the one Bull wears all the time. It says Freak on it. I've heard Bull talking to him on the phone, but he's definitely one of the members I haven't met.

I've gotten used to calling Bull by his nickname. I'm not sure I could ever call a man I care about Freak. Though when I look at him, I can't say the name doesn't fit. He has these piercings and ink, and when I say ink I don't mean just some. No, Freak is *covered* in ink. I don't think there's one part about him not inked up. Even his face has ink on it. It disappears under his collar but right before it does there's this…bullet hole, and it looks so real…it looks as if there is blood dripping from it. I jump back, quickly, barely resisting the urge to touch the tattoo. It has to be a tattoo, because if it was a real wound he wouldn't be standing here.

"Whoa, there sweet thing. You're looking a little lost," he says, putting his hands on my shoulders to steady me.

"I uh…I'm looking for Bull?"

He looks me over, before asking, "You Bull's doctor?"

"Yeah," I answer, wondering if I still am.

"Gotcha. Well, I'm late to pick up my women, so I'll see you later. Be careful in there. It's party night. Anyone comes near you, just tell them you're Bull's property."

I nod, unsure of what to say. Besides, I'm kind of speechless. Whether it's because he's late to pick up his *women* instead of one woman, or that he told me to tell people I was Bull's *property*, I couldn't say. Maybe it is a mixture of both. He holds the door open for me and I don't have a choice but to go on in.

When I'm inside, I really want to take off running back to

my car. I get mad at myself. I'm not a woman without a backbone, and I'm not about to start now. I love Bull, and I'm not a pushover. I can do this, and if Bull's not man enough to accept my apology, then I'm going to go back and enjoy a two hour bubble bath, a good book, a bottle of wine, and I'll forget all about Dorian Kane! Even as I think it, I know I'm lying. I don't want to forget Bull. *I don't think I can.*

Just inside of the door, there's a man sitting with a similar jacket but instead of a name patch like Bull's—it says nothing. Maybe he doesn't have a name?

"You been approved by the brother's? You look different than the normal chicks, and you've got way too many fucking clothes on to keep a man's interest."

I look down at my jeans, long-sleeved shirt, and then back to the man.

"I'm looking for Bull? I'm his...,"

Crap! What do I say? Girlfriend? Doctor? *Property?*

"Skye?"

I turn when I hear Bull's voice, and what I see causes physical pain. He's got a half-dressed, gorgeous woman, on his lap. Her hair is midnight black hair and so long it caresses her ass. *I'd like to hack it off, and let it cover her body, after I beat the hell out of her.* She's beautiful. I hate her, but I hate him more. *Bastard!*

"Well, I guess I'm not anything to you. Here I thought you were upset. Guess I needn't have worried. It looks like you wasted no time finding someone to take my place. Gee! Maybe that is how you operate!" I tell him. I wish I had a something to throw at him.

He just sits there with a stupid look on his face. I'd have to get closer to him to slap him, so instead, I just turn and walk out. *Asshole.*

Chapter 42

BULL

I T'S LIKE WATCHING a natural disaster. It happens in front of your eyes, and you just sit there watching, unable to tear your eyes away. I'm just sitting here like an idiot, when the woman I care most about in the world turns and walks away. When the door slams, I'm finally jarred out of my stupor, stand up, and then catch one of the Twins, before she falls. Of course, I literally shove her out of the way to get to the door.

I run to catch up with Skye. Luckily, she's standing at the door searching through her purse—muttering to herself. She pulls a key out and starts to walk away. Before she can, I wrap my arm around her, pull her into me, and guide us to the corner of the building—out of the main light. She starts kicking backwards, trying to hit me, most glance off, though she does manage to get in one pretty decent shot.

"Let me go, you asshole!"

"Careful Doc, that's almost a curse word," I goad her—which probably isn't the smartest thing in the world to do.

"Let me go, and then you can go back inside! Maybe whoever that was in your lap will use the words you like!"

"I'd rather find ways to make you say them."

"Well you're on the right track!" she huffs. Once I've moved us down to the middle of the cement block wall, I push her up against it. She starts fighting me again, peppering my chest with her small fists, and trying to push away from me. I capture her wrists with my hands, and hold them above her head.

"You need to calm down, Skye."

"You need to take a long walk off a short pier!"

"You realize that doesn't even make sense, right?" I ask her, and for some reason I'm smiling.

"It means you should go swim in shark infested waters!"

"Wow, Doc. That hurts."

She stops fighting, looks at me, and her eyes are glowing. Her face is flushed, and her hair is falling from the clip in the back.

"It didn't feel great to see some woman half-dressed draped all over you! At least you changed hair color this time! I guess you get props for that!"

"It didn't mean anything, Doc. I was getting ready to tell her to leave."

"I'm sorry my timing was so bad," she snipes back.

"God you're beautiful when you get all bitchy," I tell her and it's the truth.

"Go tell *her* that," she huffs, pushing against my hold.

"Skye, she didn't realize I'm not on the market. That's partially your fault."

"My fault?" she asks, like I'm insane.

"You don't come to the club enough to claim me in front of the Twinkies.

"Oh my God!"

"Skye, it didn't mean anything, I didn't want her. Will you calm down?"

"Gee, Bull maybe I'd believe you *if* you didn't have a hard-on!"

I look down and sure enough there's a tent going on. I should have worn my jeans, instead of my fatigues.

"That's for you."

"Do *not* treat me like I'm stupid."

"Jesus, she was in my lap, kissing on my neck. It's just a natural reaction. You'd do the same if your tits were being played with."

"I don't know. Let me go find someone to do that, and I'll be sure to let you know!"

An image of another man's hands on Skye, touching her, teasing her nipples and taking them into his mouth, flashes through my mind.

"Fuck no! That is *not* happening."

"Excuse me? Who the hell do you think you are to tell me that? Besides, what's good for the goose is good for the gander."

"Am I the goose or the gander in this scenario?"

"Fuck you! You know what I mean."

"Oh, Doc, you said fuck."

"You drove me to it! And so help me, if I let that word fly in front of Matty, I will hunt you down and kill you slowly!"

"I think I'm going to have to punish you, Doc," I tell her, letting my hand slide under her shirt. I hold my palm against the soft skin on her side.

"Oh no. We're not playing this game."

"What game, Doc?" I ask her, letting my hand drift further up, enjoying the silken warmth my hand finds.

"There's no way you get to touch me when I find you with some skank on your lap."

"I told you Doc, it was nothing. If you had been just one minute later, you would have seen that for yourself."

"I don't like it."

"So noted," I whisper in her ear, letting my hand drift to the underswell of her breast. "What were you coming here to tell me, Doc?"

"Bull! Let me go!" she demands, but I notice her fingers bite into me, instead of stopping my hand from cupping and kneading her breast—*which I do and nearly groan the feel of it.*

"What did you come here to tell me?"

"That I...what are you doing?"

"Playing with your tits. Did I tell you how much I fucking love them?"

"Oh..."

"What were you going to tell me, Skye?"

"That I...*Oh!* Don't stop doing that," she gasps, when I bend down and suck one of her nipples into my mouth. I bite it before letting go, to admire the wet spot on her shirt.

"Tell me."

"I wanted to tell you, you were right and I'm sorry."

Her words lock into place, and I reward her by sucking on her nipple again.

"Did I tell you, Doc? How I think about eating out your sweet cunt when we're apart? How thoughts of your pussy drive me wild?" I ask her, letting my lips trail up her neck, so I can whisper into her ear.

"No," she breathes, "I find it hard to believe though, considering you have Twinkies when I'm not around."

I pinch her nipple and twist it hard to punish her.

"They don't hold a candle to you, and you know it. I don't want anyone but you. I haven't since I first met you. The minute you gave me lip I knew."

"Knew what? That you're a jerk?"

I grin and take my hand away. I hear a whimper of disappointment, but she doesn't need to worry. I put a hand on each of her shoulders, then let my fingers move over the collar of her shit, following it down to the edges of the V-neckline.

"I knew you were the one I was going to claim."

I let those words sink in, and then I pull on each end of her shirt, rending it in two. The sound of the fabric tearing is drowned out by her gasp of surprise.

"What are you doing?" she asks, her nails biting into the skin on my side.

"I want to watch your tits when you suck my cock," I tell her.

"Right now? Bull? We're in public."

"Right fucking now. And when I come, you're going to swallow every fucking drop."

"No condom?"

"No fucking condom. Nothing but my cock and your warm, wet mouth. You got a problem with that, Doc?"

"No…"

"Then drop to your fucking knees, woman."

Chapter 43

SKYE

"**B**ULL..." I GROAN. I need to try and remember why I'm mad at him. I really try to, and it almost comes back to me. Then his hand pushes my shoulder, and I'm down on my knees in front of him. His hard cock is pushing against the khakis he has on.

Almost on auto pilot, I reach up and undo his belt and pants. He's going commando, not that I'm surprised. My hand cups his balls, loving the way the skin is soft, but still coarse. They are heavy with his seed. I move my fingers over his cock, tracing the veins that push against the tender skin. His cock is so thick, wide and long. The soft mocha color is just a shade lighter than his balls. It springs forth from a small, but neatly trimmed, dark patch of hair. I let my fingers play in the coarse nest. There's not a thing about his dick I would change, especially the way it curves. My hand pumps him slowly and on my downward stroke I watch as the skin slides away and reveals his wide head. It seems impossible, but it is a different hue than the rest of him.

My eyes zero in on the small crease which is covered in his pre-cum. I pump him again and this time stop on the upward thrust. Holding him taunt, I flatten my tongue against his cock and lick him, groaning as the salty taste of his skin.

213

"Fuck yeah, that's it Doc. Jesus, I wish you could see your-self right now. Is your pussy, wet for me? Does sucking me make your little clit beg for attention?"

If only he knew. I might be fooling myself, but I think he was telling me the truth about the woman in there. Still, I plan on making sure he knows what he'd be throwing away if he fucks up.

When my tongue reaches the top of his cock, I let it fan back and forth over the head before diving in, and finding that small opening, I'm starting to crave. I gather the fresh, hot pre-cum, as my hand works him by thrusting down. With his head is completely exposed, I look up at him and let him watch, as I take him in my mouth.

He's so big, I don't see any way I can fit him into my mouth completely, but I put my hand at the base of his cock. I squeeze tight, so that part doesn't feel left out. My tongue praises his cock, sliding along it, teasing, licking, and petting his dick, as I take inch after delicious inch into my mouth.

Bull's hand wraps into my hair, twisting it hard. The sharp pain does nothing but increase my desire. Up and down I fuck his cock with my mouth, working in tandem with my hand. My hand squeezes him tight, slides up, and then glides back down.

"Jesus. I love watching the way I disappear into that fuck-ing mouth. There's only one thing you're forgetting, sweetheart."

I look up, my eyes watching him in silent question—half of his cock still inside my mouth. Cum leaks out of the head and drips unto my tongue. I groan around him, at the taste. The vibration of my moan must break something loose in Bull, because that's when he takes over.

When I say he takes over, I mean it. He uses his hands on my head and he takes control. Pushing me down on his cock until the head enters into my throat. Tears slide from the corners of my eyes, as he triggers my gag reflex, before pulling me back up.

"Breathe through your nose, Skye. You can do it baby."

For some reason his praise, makes me want to do exactly that. When he thrusts his cock deep in my mouth again, I widen the stretch of my jaw and consciously relax my throat muscles. I breathe like he told me to. When he gets to my throat, I look up at him for direction.

"Work your throat baby. I want to feel you swallow and deep throat me. *I need this, Skye.*"

What is it about the man you love telling you he needs something? The plea in his voice, the need in his eyes, and his request all swirl together into a drug headier than any you could buy on the street. It's impossible to ignore. I give him what he wants, and as he fucks my mouth hard, using me. Regardless, I'm the one who feels powerful. I'm the one who feels in control. His cum jets into my mouth, and I swallow it down. When he calls out my name, as he fills me full of cum, I definitely feel like the winner. It leaks from my mouth runs down his shaft, and pools on his balls that I'm palming. In this moment I feel sexy, beautiful, alive, and most importantly—*loved.* It doesn't hurt that when he finishes emptying inside of my mouth, he pulls me from his cock, helps me to stand, and holds me tight into his body.

"I love you, Skye. You're my world, sweetheart. My world."
I let the warmth of his praise surround me.

"I love you too," I tell him, giving him the words he needs, and the ones that make me the most happy. "I love you too."

AW

I TRIED TO warn her. She wouldn't listen. I can't see what she does once she gets into that sinful compound. I can only imagine though. Why wouldn't she listen? Why is she making me do this?

My tears fall unchecked. I grieve for what she's making me do. Her sins can't go unpunished.

They can't.

Chapter 44

SKYE

"H EY BUCK. HOW are things today?" I ask, as he mops up the floor.

It's my first day back to work since the night I told Bull, I loved him. If you discount the fact that Bull's going crazy trying to figure out who rigged my brakes, life is pretty much perfect. Heck, I've not even had to deal with Dr. Reynolds or Dr. Eldridge today. I've seen them of course, it seems like everywhere I turn one of them is lurking and watching me. *It's creepy.*

"Pretty good. You doing okay? I heard about your accident while I was away."

"I know I didn't see you around last week! I'm okay, I was just a little banged up. I hope you had a good vacation though?"

"It wasn't bad. Did they find out what happened to your brakes?"

"Nothing to worry about. Probably just rusted brake lines," I lie. It's not like you want to just announce, *oh I think someone is trying to kill me!*

"Well that's good. Are you ready for Christmas?"

"Not even a little bit," I laugh. "Bull is going to pick me up here in a few minutes, when I clock out. We have a treat for

Matty."

"It's a shame you have to work. A good woman like you ought to have a man who takes care of her, so she doesn't have to worry about anything."

"I'd go crazy," I laugh telling him. "Do you have the holiday off?"

"Yeah, and I'm working up a big surprise for my girl. She'll be shocked."

"When do we finally get to meet this mystery woman? You've been talking about her for months."

"Soon. We need some alone time first. There are problems we need to work out."

"Well I hope it works out for you, and we finally get to meet this woman who has you wrapped around her finger."

"I have it all planned out. I want it to be the best Christmas she's ever had. I've been planning it for the last four months."

"What a romantic. This world needs more men like you, Buck."

"There you go flirting with other men, Doc. I just can't leave you alone," Bull says, walking up.

"Oh will you stop? I was just bragging on Buck because he's been planning his proposal to his girlfriend for Christmas. He wants to make it special."

"Hell Buck, you are going to make the rest of us men look bad."

"You find a good woman you got to make sure you take care of her. You don't want some other man to come in and steal her away."

"Amen, brother. Amen. Or you can keep her tied up in bed, unable to get away."

I slap Bull on the shoulder. "Will you hush?"

"What? I was just offering my advice."

"We better get going or we're going to be late. We're taking Matty down to Burnside Island to look at the Christmas lights."

Buck nods goodbye, and goes back to his mopping. "Have a good time then. I'll see you later."

Bull grabs my hand and we head out. He drove me to work on his bike, so he could pick me up. We're going to surprise Matty by picking him up at school, then have dinner together, and finally head off to see the lights and meet Santa Claus. The way I figure it, this will be my last year with Matty where he still mostly believes in Santa. I want to enjoy it.

Chapter 45

SKYE

"I CAN'T BELIEVE Dr. Reynolds let you come back," Dr. Eldridge says in his snarkiest voice. My hand shakes with the need to slap the hell out of him. I've been lucky, and I've not had to deal with him too much. The respite from him has been good. Bull told me he and the club were checking into people I work with, and have contact with daily. In fact, I'm supposed to go back to the club tonight, and go over surveillance video to see if I can identify anyone that was purchasing gift cards. I find myself wishing it was this guy, just for the sole purpose of watching Bull destroy him.

I don't see it happening. I don't think this guy is anyone I know personally. The very thought that I could be wrong, chills me. I want to put this behind me, and move forward. So, anything I can do to help, I will.

I do decide however, to ignore Dr. Eldridge's hissy fit. Therefore, I don't bother responding. Instead, I go back to writing in my chart, and smile at Alex, who is the floor nurse for my patient.

"Could you review the chart, Alex and make sure everything seems okay to you?" It's ridiculous that I feel the urge to do this, but I don't trust Eldridge not to go behind me and change my orders. It seems a good precaution to make.

"It's all good Skye," Alex says, and I nod, before walking around the idiot who is determined to ruin my good day.

I'm thinking of switching hospitals, Bull keeps saying no. He says his club will find who's doing this and handle it. That's another thing, he's determined whoever this is, is a man. I don't know what to think at this point, and I really don't know what he means when he says he'll deal with them. I got a feeling I don't *want* to know.

I'm anxious to leave work. Bull, Matty and I are putting up the Christmas tree. Matty loves it and I want to make sure he has a wonderful Christmas. Bull and I are pulling out all the stops to guarantee it happens. My mind is on all the things I need to do this evening. I open my locker while on auto pilot. So I'm unprepared for what happens. As the door opens, photos fall out—so many I can't count them. There are at least fifty and probably closer to a hundred of them. I pick a couple up, and at first I'm not sure what I'm looking at. It takes me a minute, and even as I'm staring at them, I don't quite believe it. My hands begin to shake, my stomach rolls, and I can feel bile rise up in my throat. All around my feet are pictures of Nurse Allen's mutilated body. *I scream.* I don't do it cognitively, I just scream.

The first one to me is Judy and she wraps her arms around me. In the distance I can hear her asking me what's wrong, but I can't talk. I can do nothing but stare a picture of Melissa's corpse. Pictures of her dead, and on the ground. *On the ground by my car!* Pictures of her naked on a cement floor. Pictures of her body slowly losing different pieces. Pictures of a bloody....bone saw... like one we use here in the hospital.

One by one my co-workers start filing in to see what the screaming was about. Clara from the cafeteria, Jake the hospital maintenance man, Dr. Eldridge, Dr. Reynolds, Judy, Ruth from accounting, Reverend Fisher the hospital Chaplin, Buck the janitor, Luke, an orderly, Alex the floor nurse, Katie a fellow resident—they all try to crowd in the room, along with Dante and Sam from hospital security. All I can think—the only thing I can grasp is...*I'm standing in a room with a murderer and I'm his or her next target.* That's when I scream again, but this time I call out the name of the one person I can trust....

"Bull!"

Chapter 46

BULL

"**Y**OU GUYS MAKE it back?" I nod to Hawk as I enter my room. He's stationed right by my bed watching over Skye—exactly where I put him when I had to leave. Until I find this fucker, I'm not leaving her alone, *not even for a minute.*

"Yeah, you can go. We're going to have Church in an hour and Skye's going to go through the surveillance tapes with Freak right before," I tell him.

"You find her?" he asks, and I rub the tension at the back of my neck. Another damn headache is forming and I can't deal with it right now. I have to be here for Doc. *I have to take care of Skye.*

"Yeah man, exactly where we thought, down by the old gravel quarry."

"Fuck."

I nod, because what the hell else is there left to say? I hated Melissa, but shit...no woman deserves what that sick fuck did to her. The only thing that makes it a little better, is that it looks like most, if not all of the truly sick shit he did, was after he killed her. Our club might take care of assholes and occasionally torture has to be used, but to do what this sick fuck did to a *woman*...this asshole has to be off his goddamn rocker.

"Okay, I'll see you in a little while man," he whispers, and then slaps my shoulder, before closing the door behind him.

I look down at the woman I love more than life, lying on the bed asleep. My heart flips over in my damn chest. When her friend Judy called and told me what happened, I busted ass to get to her. Skye collapsed in my arms and cried for a fucking hour, before crashing. She's so emotionally and physically drained. I don't want to wake her, but I don't have much choice. The sooner she watches the surveillance tape the better. We've also got files on the main suspects she needs to see. None of the pictures of our suspects match anyone on the camera footage, however. *That would be too motherfucking easy.*

"I need to call Blair," Skye whispers, and I look down at her.

"I already have, Doc. About thirty minutes ago, actually. She said Matty went to her room to rest and everything was fine. I gave her the club number if she needed us."

"I don't want him left alone, Bull. I want him with us."

"I sent Gunner over as soon as I hung up, sweetheart. Do you want me to have him bring Matty here?"

"Please? I just...*I'm scared*, Bull."

"I know, Doc. I know," I tell her, pulling her close to me when she stands and comes to me. Her scent calms me. How the fuck that is possible after the shit I just saw, I don't know. *It's just true.* I call, Gunner and ask him to go in and get Matty, bring him back here, and then hang up. I look down at Skye, trying to give her a smile, needing to reassure her. "We're going to get this fucker."

"I know," she says, and there might be fear, but I can't find a trace of doubt.

"I love you, Doc."

Now it's her time to try and smile. She fails miserably, but the way she lays her head on my chest and encircles her arms around me makes up for it. "I love you, Bull. With all my heart."

I want to stay here and just enjoy the feeling of holding the world in my hands, but I can't. Regretfully, I pull away and look down at my girl. "You ready to go look at the stuff the club has?"

"Let's get this done," she sighs.

SKYE'S JUST STARTED going through the tape with Freak, when my phone rings. I step to the back of the room so I don't disturb them and answer.

"Bull."

"Bull, it's Gunner. I went in to get Skye's boy, and man, he's not here."

"What the fuck do you mean he's not there? I told you to guard the house with your motherfucking life!" I snap. I hear a chair crash, and Doc is up, the chair she was sitting in tips to the floor and she's running to me. Motherfucker, I've let her down again. Worse, I've let Matty down. I should have picked him up at school, instead of letting Blair.

"I've been guarding an empty house, fucker. The lock on the inside of the window has been opened. Matty had to be the one to do it. There's a mud hole there too. Matty's is the only set of footprints. He had to open the window himself and climb out."

"Why in the fuck would he do that?"

"Bull what's going on? Where's, Matty?" Sky asks, desperate, her fingers claw into my chest, her body shaking.

"Hang on, Doc," I tell her, trying to concentrate on what

Gunner is saying.

"He left a note on the bed saying his friend Greg invited him over to his house for pizza and video games. I think the kid just snuck out man."

"Get your ass here now. I'll get the address from Skye and go and get Matty," I order hanging up.

"Bull?" Skye asks, tears in her eyes, and her whole body trembling. Dragon and Freak, walk up behind her.

"It's okay, Doc. Matty's just picked the worst time in history to be a kid. He snuck out."

"Motherfucker," Dragon grumbles in the background.

"Snuck out?" She cries."

"He left a note on Blair's bed saying his friend Greg invited him over for pizza and video games."

"Why would he do that? He knows better than pull a stunt like that. Oh God, Bull! He's only nine years old and what if this sick…"

I put my hand on her lips and stop her from going any further.

"Let's not borrow trouble, Doc. I'll go get him and bring him back."

"Okay," she nods and then color drains on her face. "Bull! Matty just met Greg at school. They've been talking back and forth online, but I've never let him go over there. I don't do that until I meet the parents. I don't know where they live!"

It feels like I've got fucking led in the pit of my stomach when she delivers her news.

"You don't know anything about Greg?"

"Not really. Matty said he lived like two streets down from us. I told him after the holidays we'd invite him over."

"I'll go get him. You two finish going through this damn tape. I want motherfucking answers like yesterday. There's no way I'm going to let shit happen in my fucking club again," Dragon growls, walking around us.

"How are you going to find him? You don't know…" I ask, but I'm talking to Dragon's back.

"I'll knock on every fucking door, on every fucking street anywhere near Skye's. I'll take Hawk and Dance with me to speed that shit up. Now get busy." He looks over his shoulder at Skye. "We'll get your boy, Doc. Don't you worry."

That seems to reassure, Skye, though I can still see fear in her eyes. Still, she nods, before turning to Freak.

"Let's get back at it," she whispers. The woman has so much courage. My heart swells with pride.

Chapter 47

BULL

"I DON'T RECOGNIZE one person on that tape you guys. No one looks familiar and the feed is so grainy and shadowy, I couldn't even tell you for sure if one of them is someone I know."

"I thought that might be the case. They're equipment is outdated. I can't event narrow it down with a fucking time stamp," Freak growls throwing something from his desk across the room.

"Okay let's move to the files," I tell Skye, needing to keep her focused.

"Have you heard from, Dragon?" she asks, worriedly.

"Doc, he's not even been gone an hour. Give them time," I tell her, trying to keep her calm, but inside I'm worried. I got alarm bells ringing like a fucking church tower in my head. Something is off. I know it.

Skye sits down at the small table, and picks up the first folder.

"Judy? No way. She could never do this, and besides her house burned down, she's been way too busy dealing with that."

"We need to take a second, third, and fourth look at every-one, Skye. Judy was on break about the time Melissa disappeared. Maybe she took that time off, to kill her and dispose of the body."

"I'm telling you there's no way, Bull. And besides, you're forgetting, I saw the pictures of Melissa…" she pauses to catch her breath, and I know she's remembering. Thank God, she didn't have to see it in person. *It was much worse.* "I saw the pictures, and it would take a man or a very big woman to accomplish that. Judy is *tiny.* A strong wind would blow her away."

I nod because we're all in agreement over that, I just wanted to make sure. "Okay, so the next one."

"Dr. Douche," she sighs, and it's the first time I've really felt like laughing all day. "I mean he's the one all of the signs point to, because he's definitely psychotic."

"And he might have been giving it to Melissa, but you did say she told the whole hospital about his inch worm."

"Inch worm?" she gives me a weak smile and I wink at her.

"Yeah. I mean it could be him. He just seems too…"

"Too what, sweetheart?"

"He is too bold and in your face? Like, I think he would attack first, and then try to be sneaky as hell to get out of it. He wouldn't write cryptic notes and do things in the background."

"Okay so we'll put him in the maybe pile and go to the next."

"Well, we can cross out Walter."

"Fuck, no. He attacked you."

"He's not going to jeopardize his career to do something like this, and he's too high brow. He thinks he's better than everyone else," she argues.

"You just described half the serial killers in America. My money is on, Walter-boy. He stays in the maybe pile."

"You just don't like him," she argues, putting the file on

top of Dr. Douche, as she so colorfully put it.

She goes through at least six more files, the security guards, cooks, nurses, and other doctors. We slowly rule those out. She stops when she comes on the next one.

"Buck…"

"The janitor I met the other day."

"Yeah. He's a nice guy, or seems to be. I don't know him that well, I'd have a hard time believing he was the one, but…"

"But?"

"Well, he does have access to everything and he's in charge of cleaning the entire third wing, which is where my locker is."

"So, he could get in and out without being noticed."

"Yeah," she says, sounding defeated.

"Buck the janitor just became our chief suspect then. Hand me his folder, Skye and I'll start doing more research while you go through the last one," Freak tells her.

"You know out of the thousands of employees there's not been that many files," she says, handing the folder to Freak.

"Yeah, you should have seen it before Freak and the rest of us narrowed it down, Doc."

She nods and looks up at me a little lost.

"What is it Doc?"

"I hate this. I hate suspecting that any of the people I've worked with could be capable of all of this."

"I know, sweetheart. We need to lock this down, so we can put it behind us," I tell her squeezing her hand. "Now go through the last one."

"Alex…"

"Yeah, the floor nurse on the cardiac unit."

"Why'd you choose, Alex?"

"Bull hasn't seen that file yet, actually. We just added it to the suspect list, I've only discussed it with him," Freak interjects, typing away on his computer.

"Why?" my girl asks, while I glance at the clock, wondering exactly why in the fuck we haven't heard from Dragon.

"You told Bull you'd been getting Alex to go back and double check your orders, because you were afraid Dr. Eldridge and earlier, Melissa were setting you up."

"Well, yeah. That's because I trust Alex."

"But, you said Alex hated Melissa."

"Even more than I did," Skye says.

"What was done to Melissa's body, Doc. That required a lot of hate."

Skye's fingers move over the file in thought.

"Doc?"

"You know, now that I think about it. Alex is always around. He's really quiet, but he's always around...and his locker is just beside mine, so he could slip things in mine, and no one would even notice. Heck we've been at our lockers at the same time. He probably even knows my combination."

"Wait. Alex is a he?" I ask.

"You really haven't read this file," Skye says.

"Well Freak, said...he was a nurse, so I just assumed."

"You do know that a third of our nurses are males, right Bull?"

"There goes my fantasies about naughty nurses," I grumble.

"You're such an ass," she says, but there's humor in her voice. "Besides the only fantasies you are allowed to have are playing doctor with yours truly."

I start to respond, but before I can get a chance, the door slams open. Dragon, Hawk and Dancer are there and Dragon is pissed.

"There's no fucking kid named Greg anywhere near your

home, Skye. There's not even one six streets over."

I pull my woman up, and hold her to me, trying to will my strength into her body. Her hands grasp my arms and she looks up at me. Tears are streaming down her face, and she looks so scared and frail. I feel like I've been punched in the balls.

"Bull…."

"Yeah, sweetheart?"

"Alex's last name?"

"Yeah?"

"It's Gregory."

Motherfucker.

I LOOK AT Matthew from across the room. I have him gagged, tied up and sitting in a chair. I'm almost ready to begin. I look at the saw sitting beside him. It's a shame I've been brought to this point. This is what happens when children are begot wickedly. Skye should have never let another man touch her out of wedlock. I thought I could cleanse her. But once a whore always a whore. Civilizations have been ruined by harlots. I can't allow her to ruin me. I have to keep myself clean. I can't let Skye defile me. I thought she was perfect. I truly did.

She failed me just like the others.

Chapter 48

SKYE

"OH GOD. OH God. Oh God...."

That's all I can say. I'm sitting in Bull's lap rocking back and forth, and I feel so cold. I don't think I will ever get warm again. My body feels like ice. My brain is numb. I've thrown-up until there's nothing in my stomach. The tears have slowed. Stray ones still find their way to the surface and I can feel them run down my face. I don't dry them. I feel like I'm dying. Bull wanted me to go lay down. He tried to get the club Doctor, Poncho to give me sedative. I wouldn't let him. I can't rest with my baby out there. *I can't.*

Dancer and Hawk come in Dragon's office dragging Alex. He's been beaten, his eye is bloody, his face swollen, and he's holding his ribs. I don't think, I'm up on him in the blink of an eye.

"Where is my baby? What did you do with my baby?" I scream, pounding on his chest. I feel Bull's arms going around me, trying to pull me back. My fingers latch onto the shirt that Alex is wearing, and I refuse to let go. "Give me my baby back. Oh God, please, just give me my baby back!" I beg trying to resist Bull's hold.

Bull pulls me away, but I bend double in his arms and push against him. I can drop to the floor. I don't want his comfort. I

234

don't want him near me. *I don't deserve comfort or love.*

"I'm a horrible mother. I let my baby down. Oh God, what he must be feeling right now. He has to be so scared," I mumble, and I was wrong, because the tears aren't gone. They fall rapidly, the sobs shaking my body, and I watch as they pool around me on the cold floor. *"I failed my baby…"*

"Doc, c'mon now. You didn't fail Matthew. We're going to get him back. I promise you. I need you to pull yourself together, and be strong for him. Matthew needs you strong so we can find him," Bull says, gathering me in his arms.

He has to hold me, my legs are just too weak. I look over his shoulder at Alex. He's shaking his head, still denying everything. I hate him. I want to tear him apart piece by piece. How could any human being do this to another? *To a child?*

"What kind of monster are you?" I scream. "How could you do this? Give me back my child! Give me back my son!" I'm screaming so loud, my voice cracks. I'm trying to pull away from Bull to get to Alex, but Bull doesn't let me.

"I'm telling you I didn't do this! You got the wrong man! I don't even know Dr. Walker's son!"

"You haven't been at Laurel Elementary? You didn't tell Matty your name was Greg?"

"What? No!"

"Give it up fucker, we know you gave a speech on career day at the school. We've been checking into you," Dragon growls, and I can do nothing but let my sobs shake me.

Bull turns us around so my back is to Alex and he can face him. I can't find it in me to argue. I just want Matty. *I need my son.*

"So? The hospital sent me! But I never met any of the kids. I didn't even know that Skye had a child that went there! I didn't do this! I would never do this! Why would you think it was me? I'm telling you, you got the wrong man!"

"You hated Melissa. It'd take a man with a lot of hate, to kill her like that."

"The whole fucking place hated Melissa."

"Whoever it is, is obsessed with Skye. You're always there. You even asked for a transfer up on the cardiac floor to be close to her," Bull says, revealing more information that the club had gathered.

"What? No! Not because of that!"

"Then why? What other reason would you have to transfer to that wing? You knew Melissa was one of the head nurses there. Why transfer to her floor, if you hated her so much?" Bull asks.

I'm so tired. I can't get the picture of Matty out of my head. I keep seeing him lying in bed in his turtle pajamas, with his hair all messed up. Did I kiss him goodbye? Did I tell him I loved him? I can't even remember. What kind of mother can't remember that?

"Because I wanted to be closer to Dr. Eldridge!"

"What?" Dragon asks, and the room goes quiet and my back stiffens, because even in my haze there's a hint of truth coming out of Alex's words.

"I'm gay! I slept with the man, and then he just decided to forget about me. Said coming out of the closet would ruin his career. I transferred so I could see him every day. I wanted to remind him I was there," Alex says, pushing his fingers through is hair and holding his head down. "For all of the fucking good it did. He ignores me."

"Fuck a duck," Dancer growls from behind me, and I turn to look at Alex.

"You really didn't befriend my son at school? You don't know him?" I say, and desperation is in my voice. Because if we have the wrong person then we're even further away from finding Matty than I hoped.

"I didn't do this Skye. I promise."

"Freak, who the fuck else has a connection with the school from the files that Skye picked?" Dragon growls.

"No one man. There's not one fucking connection," Freak answers, and I bury my head in Bull's chest. His hands comb through my hair, and I'm afraid the blackness is going to swallow me up when Alex speaks up.

"Buck!"

I look at him, and the room goes still.

"What the hell are you talking about?" Bull asks, his body is vibrating against mine.

"Buck! He could be the one you want," Alex says.

"The school doesn't have any record of ever having Walter there as a guest, or an employee of any sort," Freak interjects.

"Yeah," Alex agrees, "he wasn't at the school, but he was working at the courthouse, next door. He was mowing their lawns. He was sitting on the picnic tables eating lunch when I came out! I asked him what he was doing and he told me he took a part time gig to earn extra money. He wanted to buy a ring for the girl he's been seeing."

"Fuck me," Dragon murmurs. "Freak!"

"Already on it, Drag."

"I want Alex locked up in one of the bedrooms until we know he's telling the truth," Bull orders. "Put Circus and one of the other recruits on him."

Hawk takes him out, but not before he looks over his shoulder at me. "I hope you find your son, Skye, honest."

I believe him and it hurts me.

"Fuck, Drag. This Buck owns a house on the Southside of town," Freak says.

"What does that mean?" I ask. No one answers, until Bull looks down at me.

"It's out by the old gravel quarry, Doc."

"Let's load up!" Dancer orders, and the men start filing out.

"I'm coming with you!"

"Fuck no, Doc. I need all my thoughts on saving Matthew. I can only do that if you're safe."

"Bull!"

"You're wasting time here, Doc. I need to go rescue our boy. I got this. You need to trust me."

I swallow and nod once. *Bull has this.* I know he does. He and his crew have worked nonstop. They even have connections at the police, which have been ignoring the whole thing so Dragon and his crew could do what they needed to do, without worrying about legal repercussions.

"Bring our son back to me, Bull." He gives me a quick, hard kiss, before pulling away.

"I'll do it, Doc. Six, you take care of my woman. You don't, and I'll make sure you don't live to regret it."

"Got it, man." Six says, and then Bull is gone. I sink down in the chair and wait. Bull will bring Matty home to me. I know he will. He has to. *He has to.*

Chapter 49

BULL

"**Y**OU READY MAN?" Drag asks.

We're outside the main office of the old quarry. We've got the place surrounded. Gunner and Dancer have spotted Buck in the office. The fucker is laying plastic down, and preparing the room. Dancer said there's also a fucking bone saw and chainsaw in the room. So, I know what the fucking psycho is planning. I'm not about to let it happen. Everyone is in their place. Dragon, Freak and I will burst through the front door. Gunner and Dancer have the back entrance. Hawk and Nailer and some of the other prospects are minding the side entrances. *We have this.* We just need to make sure my boy doesn't get hurt in the process. *Matthew is mine.* I'm claiming him, just like I did his Mama.

"I want lead man. I want to kill the fucker before he gets a chance to hurt my kid," I tell Drag, my hands tightening and untightening on my gun.

"You got it," he says, slapping me on the back. I click the radio so the other men know.

"Approaching now. No movements until you hear my shot," I tell them, and we take off.

We advance as quietly as we can. I don't want to do anything that might tip Buck off. I hear the chilling sound of the saw starting. I kick the door open, and Matthew is bound in a chair, with a gag in his mouth. Buck is across the room, and he has just picked up the bone-saw. He is flexing his thumb on the trigger, and adjusting speeds. When we bust through he looks at us. Surprise is all over his face. I'd love to take time to extract justice out of his sorry hide, but I don't. It doesn't even occur to me.

I shoot him right between the eyes, and for once there is not a fucking tremor is in sight. I shoot once, and he falls. I walk to him, and it's a kill shot. *I know it is.* Just to make sure, I shoot him twice more in the heart. I put my gun away, and notice that Dragon, Dancer, and Freak have surrounded Matty, not letting him see the body—or what I did. I'm grateful. They move away when I get there. I hear the men in the background already moving the body. I take the gag out of Matty's mouth and pull his head as close as I can, since his arms and legs are still bound on the chair. I kiss the top of his head, like I've seen Skye do so many times.

"You okay, buddy?" I ask him, and tears are falling down my face. I don't give a fuck. My hands are trembling as I pull away. I try and dry up Matty's eyes. It has nothing to do with my injury. It's all emotion.

"I'm okay, Bull. I knew."

"Knew what buddy?" I ask him, using my pocket knife to cut the rope on his hands and feet.

Matty brings his hands around, and I rub them as the pinched, white skin, slowly becomes red again. He's crying, just like I am. But, he gives me a watery smile, just the same.

"I knew you'd come for me."

His faith and trust does something inside of me. For a second, I'm robbed of my voice.

"You did?"

"Yeah, Bull. It's what family does. We have each other's backs."

I shake my head in agreement, and catch Matty as he face plants into my chest. I wrap my arms around him and hold him tight.

"Yeah buddy, that's what family does. They have each other's backs. No matter what," I tell him, my heart full.

I look up and all of my brothers are standing around me. Dragon, Dancer, Freak, Gunner and Nailer are looking at me. My brothers. *My family.* And I know if we had called Crush he'd be right here too.

"That's definitely what family does, Matty. They have your back no matter what."

I'm a lucky fucking man.

Chapter 50

BULL

I'M A LUCKY *fucking man.*

I'm in the cage. I let Freak drive my girl home. It's not something I would have done before Skye. Now, other things are more important that my bike. Now…I want Matthew with me. Jesus I may never let him out of my sight again.

It's amazing how well he's doing. All the way back he chatters on, telling me how *'Greg'* befriended him one day at recess. He talked to the fucker every day online, right under my nose. Skye and I are going to have a long talk with him about talking to strangers. The next thing we're doing is talking to the damn school board about tightening up security. Maybe we should homeschool him? Or hell maybe private school? Fuck, maybe the club should hire a teacher to take care of our own kids? I need to talk to Dragon about this shit.

We pull up to the club and I resist the urge to carry Matthew. *Dragon's a fucking liar.* When something is precious to you, and you almost lose it? You want to hold it close all of the fucking time. *I get it now.* I know why he carries Nicole. Matthew wouldn't like it though. He wants to be a man in front of me, and I understand it. So, I let him walk beside me, but I keep my hand on the back of his shoulder. We walk to the club, he's still talking about things. I haven't talked, because fucking hell, I don't think I could find my voice. We're almost to the doors, when they are torn open. Matthew stops talking and we look at Skye. She stares at Matty and sobs break free from her. She falls down on the ground crying and opens her arms, Matty dives into them. I stand behind him watching my family in front of me. She looks up above Matty's shoulder, and the love and happiness in her eyes practically beams.

"I love you. I love you. I love you," she's repeats over and over. She's saying the words to Matty, but there's not a doubt in my mind that she's giving me those words too.

"I love you too, Doc." I whisper. She can't really hear me, but I know she sees me. I know she gets it.

I'm a lucky fucking man.

Chapter 51

BULL

"YOU DOING OKAY, Doc?" I whisper to her sometime later.

We're lying in my bed at the club. It has to be almost seven in the morning. Daylight is starting to break through the window. Skye's been in Matty's room most of the night. I finally convinced her that she needed sleep, and we could spend time with him tomorrow. She agreed, reluctantly. That was about an hour ago and I'm starting to feel guilty. I wanted to hold her, but if she's not going to rest, then…

"I love you, Bull," she says interrupting my thoughts.

I'm lying on my back, she's curled into my side. It might be my favorite way to sleep, or like now, just watch the sun come up. Her head is on my chest and I've got my fingers curled in her hair.

"I love you, too."

"Thank you for bringing our son, home," she whispers, turning her head slightly to place a kiss on my chest. The arm that she has haphazardly wrapped around my stomach tightens, and hugs me closer.

"I'd die before I'd let you or Matty go, Doc. If you aren't here, I don't have a reason to keep taking breath." Her arm flexes, once again tightening on me, and I feel moisture slide down my stomach. "Hey now, I didn't mean to make you cry!"

"I know. I'm just emotional."

"We have Matty home now, Doc. It's going to be okay."

She sits up, and before I know exactly what she has in mind, she pulls the covers out of the way and is straddling me.

"Doc?"

"How come no matter when it is, it seems your dick is hard?" she asks, her hand pinning the tip against my stomach.

Fuck! That feels good. I'm not sure anything could feel better. Even as I think it, I know it's a lie. Inside her is the sweetest heaven I've ever known.

"Because I stay hard anytime you're near me," I answer honestly. "You probably think that's a line, but it's not, Doc. Jesus, from the minute I met you, my dick has been permanently locked and loaded. I don't see that changing. I'll probably be ninety years old and chasing you around the nursing home, begging you to straddle me on my wheelchair."

She giggles, but I barely notice. Instead, my head goes back against the pillow in pleasure. My hands bite into her sweet ass, and my eyes follow her body as she moves. Skye's fixed it so my dick has the lips of her pussy spread open and she's sliding that sweet cunt back and forth on my dick—grinding and coating me in her need.

"God, Doc. You're fucking soaked," I moan, because she's drenching my cock. Her body picks up speed, her hands press into my shoulders, as she takes what she needs.

"Am I wet enough?" she pants. I can hear it in her voice, and the way her pussy spasms against my cock. She's close to coming.

"You're perfect. Let me watch you come, sweetheart please," I tell her, and I'm rewarded when her eyes open up, and she smiles down at me.

She lifts up and I grunt in disappointment, because as close as she was, I wasn't far off. Then her sweet little hand wraps around my cock and she positions him right where she wants him and slides down on me.

"Fuck. I love the way you stretch me, Bull."

She knows what it does to me to have her sweet little mouth whisper fuck, while I'm getting her off. Eventually, I'm going to have her talking dirtier than she could ever imagine. Because I know that I'm the only one who she will let go for. The only one to make her lose complete control.

"Hold onto the headboard and lean over me, Skye. *Now.*"

She does as I order, and the position brings her tits to my face and I capture one in my mouth and suck it firmly in, letting my tongue play with the hardened nipple.

"Oh fuck, that feels good. Suck harder, Bull. Bite it," she orders, and her hips are bucking as she tries to ride my cock.

This time, I do as *she orders*. My fingers bite harder into her luscious ass. I use one of my hands to explore the valley of her ass, pressing it between the cheeks, and searching out that sweet little hole. My other hand is on her hip, and controls the speed of her ride. Correction, she's not riding me. I'm making her ride me. I control her speed, and the angle my cock. I make sure I scrape her inner walls. *Every-fucking-thing, I control.* She can do nothing but accept the pleasure I give her. My fingers breech the opening in her ass. No deep, I can't do that from this angle, but enough so the extra presence spikes her pleasure.

"Fuck me. Oh God, fuck me. Fuck me. Fuck me," she repeats the words like a mantra. And I do exactly what she asks. I'm sliding her up and down on my shaft, with my fingers pushing against her ass. On each downward thrust, I grind that sweet cunt into me. I can feel my cum gathering, and I know

I'm about to blow, but I'm not about to go before my woman. Her body is convulsing and her breath is coming in hard, short gasps. I know she's there. She just needs the tiniest of pushes. So I bite down on the nipple I have trapped in my mouth.

The spike of pain, makes her scream out my name, and then she's done for. Her climax comes hard and strong. I thrust her up and down on me, she grinds the hell out of her cunt, using me without realizing it. Her sweet cream covers my shaft, she bucks and yells out the word fuck as she rides me harder than any rodeo queen.

Watching her and seeing her pleasure, combined with the way her greedy pussy is sucking on my cock, sends me over the edge. I shout as I unload inside of her, coating her womb. She drains me dry, and when it's over she collapses against my body. I'm still buried inside of her, our combined juices are running down her thighs. Her head rests to my shoulder and she kisses my neck.

"I think I can sleep now."

"Do you want to…?"

"Just like this Bull. Feeling your cum and you inside of me. This is exactly how I want it," her tired voice says. "I love you, honey," she yawns.

I think she's out before she can hear me tell her I love her too, but as she snuggles into me and squeezes my cock in her sleep, I figure she knows. If not I'll be sure to show her later. I fall asleep with a smile on my face, and my cock in the only place in the world it *ever* wants to be.

Chapter 52

SKYE

"I CAN'T BELIEVE we're opening presents in the middle of the Savage clubhouse. My balls are never going to unshrivel man. Do you know how the mighty have fallen here?" Gunner whines.

I notice the other men are flipping him off, and the women are laughing and ignoring him.

"My balls are shriveling too!" Matty pipes up, because in the week since Bull and the club rescued him, Matty has decided he wants to be just like the men here. *There are worse things that could happen.*

I shoot a look at Gunner, and he actually blushes. Then I have to look down, because I don't want everyone to see me laughing along with them. Matty is on cloud nine. He hasn't even had a nightmare in the weeks following his kidnapping. In fact, he's in his element. Crusher and Dani came in for Christmas with her new adoptive son, Dakota. He's the same age as Matty and they've instantly connected. For so long Matty has missed having a male influence in his life and now...

I look around and Dragon, Dancer, and Crusher are sitting at a table laughing and drinking a beer. Gunner, Hawk, Nailer and Six are all standing around them laughing. Nicole, Carrie, Dani and some new girl everyone call's Lips are all at a table holding babies, and joking. Lips apparently just came home and is engaged to Six. Freak is in the corner, holding the woman he just got engaged to, Nikki, and I can only think that I was wrong.

I worried Bull and his lifestyle was the wrong choice for my life. But he was right. *He was right all along*. Here is a real family, of really good people, and every single one of them would lay their lives down for my son, for me and for Bull. *I get it*. I'm blessed to be part of them.

I feel Bull's arm snake around my stomach, as he pulls me back into him.

"What are you thinking, Doc?" he whispers in my ear.

"How grateful I am that you made me and Matty part of your crazy family," I tell him honestly.

He places a kiss on the inside of my neck. "I love you, Doc."

"I love you too."

"All right brothers it's time for some Christmas around here," Dragon orders. "Freak, since you jumped the gun and already gave your woman her present, how about you give them out?"

"Got it Boss-man," Freak says, and he gives Matty and Dakota some presents from Santa. New game systems. Apparently the latest and the best, according to Bull. The boys immediately start planning on how they can play with each other even though they live apart.

While I was distracted watching the kids, it appears all the couples have paired off. Nicole is now in Dragon's lap. Carrie is in Dancer's and Dani is in Crusher's. The others including Lips and Six have all moved to another table, and Freak has already given them boxes to open.

Gunner holds up this long white and red striped knitted

rectangle like thing. It's about six inches in length and at its base is two oval like shapes knitted in green. Gunner's waving it around.

"What the hell is this, Nicole?" he asks.

She looks up at him and says. "A umm...bird warmer. Prevents shriveling."

The room rocks with laughter.

"Dad? Why does Gunner need a bird warmer?" Dakota asks Crusher.

"I'll explain later, boy," he says.

"Yeah, like when he's forty," Dani mutters.

Crusher kisses her while laughing, "I love you, Hellcat."

"Love you too, Cowboy," she responds, holding him close.

Freak brings two boxes to Dragon and Nicole.

"You first, Mama," Dragon orders.

Nicole opens up her box and pulls out a gold chain, but the attached pendant is what is breathtaking. It's a perfectly, precisely cut dragon that's made of beautiful emeralds and right in its chest is a dark ruby, in the shape of a small heart.

"Dragon," Nicole cries, wrapping her arms around him.

"You're always my heart, Mama. Forever."

"Open yours!" she urges.

Dragon opens the box, and he's quiet. I can't help but wonder what's in there. Then he pulls out a yellow baby rattle.

"Fuck...Mama..." he says, and then stops. When he looks up, his eyes are glowing, but I see something in the man I never thought I would see. *Fear.* "You will not get sick, Mama. You will not die on me Nicole. You will listen to every fucking thing I tell you, and you will be healthy. You hear me?"

"Yes, Dragon. I hear you. It'll be fine sweetheart, and you'll be with me every step of the way this time."

"Damn straight," he says gruffly, and then he kisses her.

It's not a small kiss either. It's the kind of kiss that even makes me hot watching. I suddenly feel like I'm intruding.

Freak has handed Dancer and Carrie a box. He apparently got her a locket with a picture of him and his sister and Carrie all together from years ago, inside. Carrie is crying, even as Dancer opens up his box. Inside are keys to a brand new Harley. The custom paint job is a Savage MC emblem with Dancers name in white and highlighted by blue flames. Carrie is rich it seems, but I get the feeling Dancer could care less. I look over at Crusher and Dani. They've already exchanged. Dani's holding her hand up and she's got a ring on that looks like the shape of a cat. I don't know what she gave Crusher, but whatever it was, he's practically making out with her. So, he must be happy. These Savage boys apparently aren't shy in public, that's for sure.

Then Freak comes to me and Bull. My stomach rolls with nerves. I think he will love what I got him. But then, you never know.

"Open it, Doc."

My hand shakes as I tear the wrapping off of the small box, and open it. Inside is the prettiest diamond that I've ever seen. He takes the box from my hand, and puts the ring on my finger.

"Will you marry me, Doc?"

"Fuck, yeah." I whisper through the tears, giving him the word he loves to wring from me the most, right before he claims my mouth.

When we break apart, Gunner is moaning again.

"Jesus H. Christ, that's three of you in one holiday!"

I dry my tears and Freak looks up.

"There wasn't a box under the tree for Bull."

"I got everything I need." Bull says, smiling down at me.

I take a step back, grinning. "I hope you have room for one more gift from Matty and me," I tell him.

Matty walks over and he has the envelope I gave him earlier. I asked him to keep it with him. I knew I could trust him, because this is just as important to him as it is to me.

"Bull," his little voice says, starting out wobbly. "Mom and I wanted to give you this together," He reaches the envelope to Bull.

Bull looks at me and then Matty, confused. He takes the envelope, his hand ruffling Matty's hair. "Thanks little dude."

He opens the envelope and unfolds the papers inside.

"What..." he stops and he looks at both of us and his eyes are dark with emotion. I think I can see tears shining in them. My nerves go away.

"We want you to be my new dad," Matty tells him, and I can hear the nerves in his voice. "Mom says if you sign the papers it will be all legal and everything. I can even have your name and stuff."

Bull doesn't respond, he looks at the papers, and then back at me. This time the tears in his eyes fall.

Matty must get worried about Bull's silence. "I mean it's cool if you don't want to or whatever, we just thought, maybe you would like to be..." He looks up at Bull confused. "Don't you want to be my dad?"

Bull tries to talk, but has to stop and clear his throat.

"Absolutely, Matthew. I want that more than anything in the world," he says, picking him up and holding him tight.

I look at my two favorite men in the whole world, crying and laughing. All of the rest of the members come up slapping Bull on the back, congratulating him, then hugging me. My eyes lock onto Bull's and he gives me everything I have ever wanted in one sentence.

"I love you, Skye."

The man I was worried would be a mistake I would never recover from? That man has become my reason for living.

"I love you too, Bull. *I love you too.*

The End and Merry Christmas
From the Savage Family.

Turn the page for a sneak peek of my new book Captured. Coming your way, January 7th.

Chapter One

Five Years ago
Raven Hills, Georgia

Skull

I get what I want. If I have to work a little harder for it?
It'll be that much sweeter.

I DON'T KNOW what it is about her. I fuck a lot of women. I'm serious, I fuck *a lot* of women. As President of the Devil's Blaze MC, I have a stable of women. I don't even particularly have a type. Skinny, curvy, firm asses, asses with some cushion to slap, big tits, a handful, small, *it just doesn't matter.* I've fucked them all and enjoyed them all. Still, when I see her standing on the street in that summer-white sundress, with her shoulders bare and the white-gold, blonde hair lying gently on her pale skin, I'm bowled over. It's like something out of a damned movie. The wind blowing just right, the way her hair slides along her face landing against those pale pink lips and just like that I am mesmerized by her.

I have shit I need to be doing. The club has a major arms deal that is trying to go south. I need to have my head in the game, but one fucking look and I have to have her. So instead of working I find myself following her into a small coffee shop and internet café on the corner of Main Street. Raven Hills, Georgia is a small town, barely a blip on the radar and that's what makes it so great for Devil's Fire. Nothing comes in and out of this town that I don't know about it. Well there might be a small exception, because I've never seen this woman before.

I stand by the door, ignoring the hush that comes over when I enter. I'm used to that shit. Every person here knows who I am and what that could mean. I'm a twisted fucker, but I like it. Hell, I relish it. Empires are built on fear. She orders a coffee and cinnamon roll and then takes her order and goes to the main back of the room. My eyes never leave hers. She fails to notice me, then again she doesn't notice that the whole damn room is watching her. There's a few men here I may have to kill. I don't care if I haven't spoken one word to her yet. For now, she's mine.

I let her get settled, watch as she sips that first taste of coffee and closes her eyes in response. I want to see that look on her face when it's my lips she tastes. She takes a bite of her cinnamon roll and I can almost hear the small sigh of pleasure from the taste. Her face looks as if she is in heaven from just one taste and right then is when I decide. I want that look on her face. That look when it's my dick she's tasting. I walk to her, because I can't *not* do it. I stand by the table and she begins giving me her eyes. Holy hell, I didn't even know they made eyes that color. Blue, but no blue I have seen before. The color of a summer sky in the heat of the day. Warm, crystal, breathtaking blue and I want them to *stay* on me.

Her eyes move slowly up my body. I know what she sees. Scarred, inked, pierced, I have miles on me. Miles that have hardened, jaded and made me a cold bastard who hides behind an easygoing persona. My men see the real me. Some respect me, all fear me and I'm good with that.

She's a princess and I'm no one's idea of Prince Charming,

so there's a small part of me that feels like I shouldn't touch her. She's pure, sweet and innocent. I watch as her hand comes up and she uses her finger to slide a small dollop of white icing that escaped to corner of her lips. She is not small, her curves move in all the right places and her breasts are heavy and I have the urge to slide my dick in between the valley that is visible at the top of her dress. So, yeah—I'm not walking away from her.

"Hello," her soft voice almost whispers. My eyes are drawn to the icing just sitting on the pad of her index finger. I want that to be me on her fingers—my cum she is currently sliding between her lips and sucking clean. Somehow, my dick grows even harder against the zipper of my jeans.

"Mi cielo," I answer sliding into the seat across from her.

She looks confused for a minute and then a small smile breaks on her lips.

"Have a seat," she mocks, as I lean back and watch her. We're quiet for a few minutes before she finally shakes her head and asks, "Can I help you?"

"Just taking in the view."

"I see," she sighs and looks unhappy. I don't like her frowning, even as I admit that little indention she gets in her forehead is cute.

"Is something wrong?"

"I was enjoying my breakfast. No offense, I don't really want company."

"No offense taken," I return easily sitting up a little straighter and putting my arms on the table, leaning in so our faces are closer together. I smile as her eyes dilate.

"This means you should leave?" She says it like it's a question and I grin.

"But, mi cielo, I am not just company."

"You're not?" She asks, watching as my finger moves to her roll. I twirl my finger in the glazed icing. Her forehead creases again, showing her irritation. I was right, it is cute.

"Of course not."

"Then what are you?"

"I am your future," I tell her honestly, bringing my finger to my mouth. My eyes lock with hers as I let my tongue slide around to lick off the creamy confection. I use just the tip of my tongue dragging it slow and teasingly along my finger, my eyes watching her the entire time before I finally suck the digit completely in my mouth, letting a moan of appreciation hum softly.

She bites into her lip and I can tell through the thin white dress she's wearing that her breathing has picked up. She's not immune to me and that pretty much decides her fate.

"I was eating that," she grumbles, pushing it away. She tries to sound pissed, but in her voice I detect a note of excitement and it's that sound that calls to the animal in me I keep hid.

"I can give you something else to eat," I tell her and we both know I'm not talking about anything on this table. I can see the moment recognition flares in her eyes.

"Do you know who I am?" She asks, her face tilting to the side.

"Not yet, but I will."

"Be careful what you ask for," she says cryptically and it makes me smile. She's a sweet little lamb baiting the big bad wolf and she doesn't even know.

"I think I can handle anything you send my way."

"Are you always so…."

"Asombroso?"

"Asombroso?" She repeats, slightly butchering the Spanish word with her sweet, southern accent.

My madre was Spanish. I look nothing like her or her family, with the exception of my dark hair. I am my father, the fucking bastard made over. Still, having been raised by my mother, words slip out from time to time. The woman in front of me inspires them. Spanish words are more lyrical, more soothing and that is what she reminds me of. She soothes something inside of me.

"The man of your dreams," I paraphrase.

"I hate to rain on your parade Casanova, but I have to leave. I'm late," she says getting up and gathering her trash in her hands. I take it from her, I'm no one's idea of a gentleman, but I have my moments.

"And where are you off to? Is there a man I should know about?"

"A man?" She asks and then it as if a light goes off and she smiles. "And if there were?"

"I'd have to have him taken care of," I tell her honestly. I leave it to her to wonder what that means. If I tell her that no one gets in the way of what I want? What would her reaction be?

"You're just a tad over the top creepy, aren't you?" She says, moving away from me. I let her go. I can see the curve of her ass sway under her dress, as I follow her out onto the street.

"Same time tomorrow mi cielo?" I ask when it becomes apparent she is intent on ignoring me. My question makes her stop and she turns around to look at me.

She studies me for a minute and those damned blue eyes are sparkling with laughter. I'd like to keep that look on her. A second later I decide I really want to know what those eyes are like when I'm slipping deep inside of her, her legs wrapped around me. I definitely want to see that look.

"Sure knock yourself out," she shrugs and turns to walk off again.

"You better be here Dulces," I tell her and there's no mistaking the order in my voice.

She turns to fully face me. On the street in the middle of the day it as if we are having a show down and perhaps we are, but I'm going to win. She needs to accept it.

"And if I'm not?" She asks and I like the spunk she's showing. A woman with fire will warm a man at night.

"I'll come find you," I answer deadly serious.

"You don't even know who I am."

"Doesn't matter."

"You could be asking for trouble."

"I like excitement."

She studies me for another few minutes and then, much to my surprise gives in. "I'll be here."

I like that she gave in, I do not like the note of sadness in her voice. I'll have to replace that with moans of excitement. I watch her until she walks out of sight and then turn back in the direction of my bike. She's going to be a challenge. I can't wait.

Author Links

Facebook:

www.facebook.com/JordanMarieAuthor

Pinterest:

www.pinterest.com/jordanmarieauth

Twitter:

twitter.com/Author_JordanM

Goodreads:

goodreads.com/author/show/9860469.Jordan_Marie

Newsletter:

http://eepurl.com/barBKv

Amazon:

www.amazon.com/Jordan-Marie/e/B00RY72I2U

Webpage:

jordanmarieauthor.com

CPSIA information can be obtained
at www.ICGtesting.com
Printed in the USA
LVHW05s1020310818
588771LV00020B/1237/P